Bernard Ashley

High
Pavement
Blues

Penguin Books

PENGUIN BOOKS

Published by the Penguin Group
27 Wrights Lane, London W8 5TZ, England
Viking Penguin Inc., 40 West 23rd Street, New York, New York 10010, USA
Penguin Books Australia Ltd, Ringwood, Victoria, Australia
Penguin Books Canada Ltd, 2801 John Street, Markham, Ontario, Canada L3R 1B4
Penguin Books (NZ) Ltd, 182–190 Wairau Road, Auckland 10, New Zealand

Penguin Books Ltd, Registered Offices: Harmondsworth, Middlesex, England

First published by Julia MacRae Books 1983
Published in Puffin Books 1984
Reprinted in Penguin Books 1990
1 3 5 7 9 10 8 6 4 2

Printed and bound in Great Britain by
Cox & Wyman Ltd, Reading
Filmset in Palatino (Linotron 202) by
Rowland Phototypesetting Ltd,
Bury St Edmunds, Suffolk

For my sons

Chapter One

Say 'misery' to me and my mind shoots straight back to Thames Reach Market, around half-six on a January morning, setting up the stall in the freezing dark. It's a sort of yardstick I've got to measure misery by. I think about it, and I reckon things are either better than that, or worse; and then I know where I stand.

It was so miserable you couldn't help feeling like a saint by breakfast time. Down there the council's kept a patch of old cobbles with a curve of tramline in it, just to give the place a touch of history – and a black wind comes rushing off the river like a death blow. Which made pulling a stall up that icy slope and hauling it on to the High Pavement single-handed – when Nick and the rest were still sleeping off Friday night – worth at least ten points on God's balance sheet of good and bad. Put that together with being up against the mouth and the boots of Alfie Cox on the next pitch and you begin to understand what being a martyr's all about. Another man with me would have made all the difference, but when you're still at school and on your own you're fair game for being baulked and pushed – turned over, even, one eye-watering winter morning. So Saturdays were never anything to look forward to: freezing ankles, grazed skin, aggravation: and that Big Ben Repeater, like any alarm clock set to go off in the middle of the night, deserved all the bouncings on the floor it got.

But it was facing it alone that was the hardest. I could have had the best set of mates in the world, but they'd need to be family to be involved in anything like that. And that we were short on – family.

'The Saturday Brat' Alfie called me, and it wasn't just the 'Brat' that was meant as an insult. To an everyday, year in, year out lot like him and his father being a 'Saturday' is the lowest of low. 'Old Mother Pin-money' he called Max, my mother. But we were just as determined as they were not to give in. She could never make enough on her leather gear to be about all the week – not like them with their van loads of this and that for hawking round the different markets – but we'd had our licence at Thames Reach as long as they'd had theirs, and our Saturdays meant every bit as much to us as their weeks did to them. The trouble was, after having their big double fronts Mondays to Fridays in all the other markets, it came hard to them to cut themselves back to just the one stall on their best trading day of the week. I suppose you could understand it. Also, the more you get, the more you want – so all they wanted was to run us off with our home-made goods and get the double Saturday licence for themselves.

But that sort of hatred is a terrible thing to live with, even on Saturdays only. It curls your fingers into a fist, it seeps into your body, it gets into your bones with the living marrow. And it's not the everlasting smell of the leather or the dye or the glue that turns you over inside, it's the conflict. And the worst of it is, you never get used to it. It's a feeling of sickness that's always there, always gripping at you. I grew up hating Saturdays like some people hate school.

'Kev! Kevin! Did you hear that alarm?'
'Yeah, I heard it.'
'Is that the time? Where's the night gone? I'd only just lost myself.'

Max's room was next to mine, and when she dropped her voice to moan to herself I heard it better than when she shouted in her top register.

'Are you making tracks?'
'Yeah.' Making plans for when I was rich, more like. Making promises about lying-in for three days at half-term. The comfort of that warm bed! Why is it beds are at their best when you've got to get out of them? They say babies catch their breath when they're born out into the cold. They say it's one of the biggest ever shocks to the human system. Well, that doesn't surprise me a bit. I had it every Saturday morning for the best part of two years. The jerk of the alarm, the cold of the floor, the pain of the kitchen light – and already the churning up inside, even before the clank of the kettle under the tap. Yanked bawling into the world of the hated routine. Then tea, sweet and too hot to hold,

and the usual words clutched around her like the faded old dressing gown she wore.

'You gonna be all right on your own?'

''Course I am.'

'You sure?'

''Course I'm sure.'

'I'll get a bit of breakfast for half-seven.'

I should live that long! 'Right. See you.' And I'd pick up the cardboard box of lamps, take a first and last gulp of tea, and go.

We weren't far from the market. We had a first floor flat a couple of hundred yards away in one of those crumbling old streets where the houses hold one another up – the sort of place you'd hate to think of as your home for ever. Although being army we felt like that everywhere: pig-sty or palace you always live a suitcase sort of life when your father's a soldier.

All the stalls were kept in the market yard at the back of Tesco's, nudging and elbowing in the wind like kids lined up in the playground. The owners had their names burned into them with pokers or sprayed on with aerosol, and my first quick look as I ran round the corner was always to see if Cox's was in there. Most of his pitch was set up off the back of his van, reversed up tight to the High Pavement, but he always had enough stuff to overflow on to his hand stall. Which meant that if it was still there, I'd made it before them: but an empty space meant they were round on their pitch already: I was too late, and I'd have all the hassle of trying to fit mine in between them and old Barnwell. Alfie Cox was an old hand at leaving cartons of saucepans and great stacks of crockery in our space while he got sorted out; and if I tried to shift their stuff myself he'd start shouting and swearing about what an impatient little Saturday Brat I was. So I went early, waking up before the alarm even some days, to get in first. But there was nothing could stop that pain of hatred in my guts.

Alfie Cox was a couple of years older than me, chucked out of school for beating-up a teacher, and fancying himself as a hard man. They reckon he was lucky not to have been put away, but even inside he'd have got a kick out of keeping people under his thumb. He was a wing-puller, a cat booter, one of life's tormentors. And good-looking as hell. His pretty face with that look of just-held-back violence was one of the reasons I had to have my breakfast *after* the early morning aggravation. There was no keeping anything down before. And there was something else about him which made that feeling worse. I had a secret on him. Something his old man didn't know: the till-racket he had going, raking off takings to line his own pocket. It was clever, I'd seen him do it, I knew how he worked it – but I hadn't got the guts to tell anyone. I could have driven a wedge between them, but I was too scared to use it. So I was just as ashamed of being chicken as I was of being frightened of him. Worse still, in a stupid sort of way I hoped Max would never spot it, because then she'd guess that I'd spotted it, too, and she'd know what I was made of. It was all so *complicated*, and none of it helped the churning up inside.

Every Saturday I wondered what he'd do next to wind me up: and that morning he'd got me with the lights. All along the High Pavement there's a line of lamp posts about twenty metres apart; but a different sort of lamp post; instead of rising up to swan-neck into street lamps these posts stop short in square metal platforms with little sloping roofs on top and a dozen plug sockets underneath. That's how they get electricity to those shaded lamps over the stalls. Four or five people share each post: each socket has got a painted number, and everyone's supposed to know which one is which. It goes without saying that Alfie had tried the obvious trick before, plugging his lights into our socket and forcing us to make a fuss – anything for a bit of aggravation – but today he'd gone that step further. I should have known he'd got something clever up his sleeve because everything else was just too normal for words.

There was no Coxes' stall in the yard, and I pulled ours out with my head down like some pit pony with the miseries, through the gate and across those awkward cobbles, the metal-rimmed wheels clattering and crunching without a millimetre of give, shooting the shock straight up my arms. I heaved the thing up the pavement steps and manoeuvred it round everyone else's stock with my legs starting to feel like they do at the finish of a push-start. And all the time I was cursing at being there too late. They were definitely there before me, and they'd have their stuff all over our pitch. They'd pretend not to see me for ages, and then they'd start to take their time. I knew their style all right. So I thought I was still in bed dreaming when I saw it all open and empty, as if they'd suddenly turned friendly. And sure enough, there they were, Alfie and his old man building up their display, minding their own business with no loud remarks, and no crates handy for back-heeling accidentally under my wheels. Of course, I knew it was too good to be true, really. You're not dreaming when your hands and feet are so freezing cold – and when a voice keeps telling you all the time that people don't turn inside out overnight. But all the same, it did look hopeful.

The two of them went on with their build-up as if I didn't exist: Alfie Cox looking like a choir-boy with his West End hair cut, just his mouth twisted as if his spit was poison: and Charlie in a meaty Lonsdale sweater, his out-door face all smooth and hard, his body taking no notice of the perishing morning as if it just refused to let a cough or cold anywhere near him.

A real tough pair. Although I've got to admit it: while I begrudged every breath Alfie drew, I had more than a bit of respect for the old man. As far as Charlie Cox's selling went – and only as far as that, mind – he was a star in his way. He was one of those market performers the crowd stands round to watch whether they want to buy anything or not: a real entertainer, better than the telly, with a terrific line in dead-pan jokes and a showman's hands that could make a cheap pen come out of a box looking like something from Hatton Garden. Just to see him produce a saucepan, hold it up, bang it with a coin to show how it wouldn't dent or scratch, then bully or sweet-talk the crowd into wanting it, was like watching a real artist. 'Who 'as a wash?' he'd ask out of nowhere, selling shower heads. 'Ever 'ave a wash, girl?' That'd get them laughing: then he'd go on to make his tinny shower heads sound such a bargain – a real give-away, a favour he was doing them – they were letting him down not to buy one. 'All done?' he'd ask, pulling this face. 'All *done*? You must be joking! 'Ere, put 'em away. They don' know good nicked gear when they see it!' He was sunny, then thundery, called all the men 'young man' and all the women 'girl'; and they loved it, put off their shopping while they stayed to watch him; and I'd stand there myself like a rabbit with a snake, and have to kick myself sometimes to remember what a threat he was to us.

So I got the stall in without any bother. I put the chocks under and let the front flap down. I untied the rolled-up canvas to take it across the top, and unlashed the lighting battern to hang it over the counter. I screwed in the special lamps and finished off by running the lead to the lamp post and plugging it in. For once in a lifetime everything seemed to be going the way it should – the way it did for everyone else. So where was the catch? I asked myself. When were things going to go wrong?

I flicked the switch. Just then, was the answer. The lights were dead. I'd plugged in, switched on, and nothing! None of the usual brilliance throwing itself back at me from the shop window opposite. I swore, I jiggled the plug about, I shook the lead; but there was nothing. It was as dead as a set of Christmas tree lights after twelve months of tangle in a cupboard.

By then a light of another sort was beginning to dawn on me, but I tested everything to be sure: the switch, the holders, the lamps. The Coxes' lights were on, so it couldn't be the supply: and by pushing my plug into old Barnwell's on the other side and seeing our lights come up like the Southend switch-on, I knew it wasn't our battern. It was the socket in the lamp post. One socket out of twelve, and it had to be ours! I looked closer, squinted into the oblong slits by Barnwell's borrowed light – and there was the unmistakable glint of crumpled silver paper shoved up inside. Alfie's chewing gum wrapper. We'd been fused, by an old and dangerous trick that could have killed me.

'Wassup, Saturday? 'Aving a spot o' trouble?' Alfie Cox was standing underneath, staring up like the golden boy looking at heaven.

'Leave 'im. You got plenty to do.' Charlie Cox didn't even look up from positioning his working box, the one he thumped with his hand. Like a lamb, Alfie wandered away: but then he didn't need to say any more. I'll never run short of little tricks, his cocky back was telling me. Why don't you just pack it in?

I know how people come to kill. It's not so much the aggro as frustration. The anger rises up inside you like an oil gush, but it

12

gets capped off by fear. If I could've jumped down off that post and thumped Alfie without getting murdered myself, I'd have done it. If my old man had been there we could have taken them both on and sorted it, with boots and fists and heads. But on my own I was useless, and instead of throwing a punch all I could do was feel my gorge rise in my throat and start thinking about weapons. Knives. Guns. Bombs.

But I thought I did well. 'Bloody nuisance!' I said, keeping my voice all light, not too worried, and I pulled the plug out of Barnwell's socket. I jumped down off the post and shouted to old Barnwell as he came puffing along with his groceries. 'Got to sort my lights out.' I even whistled something as I sauntered off to report the fault to the Market Superintendent, just like someone a little bit annoyed by a small setback. But inside me that capped-off pressure was doing all sorts of damage, and the whistling wasn't really whistling at all but a series of short bursts because frustration had taken my breath. I'd kill them. I would. One day. Something had to be done to them. I turned the corner out of sight and ran to the Superintendent's office – and I was inside and opposite his electric fire before I realized the tune I'd been murdering. 'Killing Time'! A dead give-away, if they'd known it: and not just because of the title. It was something my old man played like no one else in the world.

'Shut the door, then. What can I do for you?' He always said it as if he doubted there was anything. Simple Saunders had all the bluster of a drill sergeant, strong with the weak and weak with the strong. He'd answer Max or me in a very different tone to the one he'd use with a borough councillor, one of the gods who walked his earth.

'It's the lights. The post. Our socket's fused.'

'What, you put a wet plug in it?' He hardly looked up from his *Mirror*.

'No, it was dry as a bone.'

'Must be your lights, then. Everything was all right last night. Overloaded it, that's what you've done. You will go over the top with your wattage.' He looked up, watery eyes through dusty glasses, licked his thumb to turn a page of the paper.

'No we haven't. It's the same as always. They light all right

13

off Barnwell's socket.' It didn't matter how churned up I was, I still had to keep my cool. It'd be no good saying a word against the Coxes to him. 'I think there's something up inside.'

He flapped his paper down. 'Mr Barnwell to you. And don't you go poking up inside that standard. I'll ask the electrician to give it a look Monday. I'm too busy today.' He lifted his paper again. 'And you remember them regulations. No paraffin lamps, sonny, and no double plugs.'

'All right, I know. You'll do it Monday, then?'

'I'll report it. *Ask* the electrician. I'm not his guv'nor you know.' He picked his nose to show he'd finished giving me his attention.

'Thanks a million.' I walked out, deliberately left his door wide open to the wind, and cut my way through the market back home to the breakfast I still wouldn't be able to get down. Not a brilliant start. Another layer of killer acid laid down inside. If only the Big Fellow was there to take these people on, I thought: if only the army had never put a cornet in his mouth. Things would be very different now.

He went so suddenly it was like an unexpected death. One day he was there, one of us, talking, eating, watching the telly, with a third share in the bathroom; and the next he was gone, leaving an old pair of shoes under the bed and a shaving stain on the towel. But with a death you clear up afterwards, you throw things out, write to people. You don't when someone goes off. You expect them back any time, coming through the door looking a bit guilty, so you make excuses, you half believe them yourself – till time tells you at last that they've gone for good; and people have guessed by then. The pain's the same as a death, though; well, it's different because it isn't so final, which cheers you up one minute; but it's *chosen*, which depresses you the next.

What it shows you, when you can think about it later without wanting to cry, is how much on his own a man is. He can be part of a family, part of an army, part of all sorts of things with other people, but inside he's just himself, sitting there thinking all those private things over on that other side of the cornflake packet. He says things he doesn't mean, does things he doesn't

14

like, goes along with things he doesn't believe in. And it's all some sort of an act; because when you come down to it we're all on our own. We do our dying on our own, and I suppose that ought to give us the clue: but for a lot of the time we fool ourselves and other people that we're all part and parcel of something else. Watch someone you love go off, and you see the rubbish of that. Think how few of your private thoughts you'd be glad to tell anyone else. That's inside your head, and inside your head is *you*. Alone. That's the way I saw it.

I used to think he was great, the Big Fellow. The best dad in the world, one of those straight-up people, I reckoned. Not like Nick's, drunk and soppy one night, clouting him the next. Always the same even temper, never in a flap. If he said 'no' today, he'd say it again tomorrow; you could bank on it, you knew where you stood. You could only get round him if he wanted you to, if it was part of his plan. But if he said 'yes' he held to that as well: no 'bones in his leg' or suddenly having something more important to do. For nearly fifteen years he was the greatest bloke alive. He played football over the park with me till it was too dark to see the ball, he talked to me like another grown up, and he gave me a look at the world from on top of his shoulders not many other kids could ever have. And above all that I felt like a fan about his talent.

Because his talent really was *something*. The army brought it out, he reckoned, and the army polished it. They shoved a cornet into his hand in the cadets, and when he showed some promise the professionals made him into a musician. After he'd signed for the full stretch he was auditioned for the Royal Artillery band where he stayed for something like twenty years. He had band tours, concerts, did instrumental teaching in the local schools and he played at weekend dances – the musician's life without the risk, he called it – and he came out on a pension while he was still young enough to make a fresh start with it. The worst he had to worry about was losing his lip or his number one shoes. Other service kids I knew hardly slept nights while their fathers did a tour in Ireland or got sent to the Falklands, but the only thing which ever disturbed my dreams was a blown-out trumpeter crawling home in the early hours of a Sunday morning.

So when he went it came as a bigger shock than anyone could ever imagine.

It happened about six months after he'd turned in his uniform and set us up with the market stall of leather goods Max made. For him I suppose it was what some people would call pure Hollywood. Psychologists might call what he did a natural reaction. I think if I'd known how to read the signs even I might have seen the writing on the wall: they were there to see. After all, what had he been? Lead trumpeter, always in the spotlight, standing up in his number ones to take the solo spots; bouncing bugle calls off the Royal Artillery front as if he owned it, taking encores at a hundred halls and bandstands up and down the country; the tall soldier in a stage-red jacket who could close his eyes and take people's breath away with his silver trumpet. What a come-down to drive parcels round London after that! What a nose-dive! And although he kept his lip with a bit of practice and he did the odd dance band date on a Saturday we should have seen when he went all quiet how much he missed his performing – and hated the end of the applause. But Ireland was Ireland; people died in Ireland; and when Ireland was the next tour of duty, with it all coming to a head again, Max was only acting for the best when she finally got him to do it. Come out and be safe.

And be sorry, as it happened!

One of the claims to fame our run-down corner of London had was an old variety theatre which never got given over to bingo or a supermarket chain. Because of the garrison with all its bored squaddies miles from home, live shows had gone on at the old Empress years after most places had closed down, and even into the 'eighties it was a well-known spot for jazz music. Telly killed even that in the end, but for a while, while I was growing up, all the big name groups got down there on Sunday nights. The three of us went there a lot – and about every three or four weeks the Big Fellow would guest in the front line for a couple of numbers. And he always got that special sort of respect only a real pro gives to another. He was so good some nights we all walked home ten feet tall. He had a sound all of his own, really effortless and natural, a mixture of a just-off rhythm and a strong blowing that was somehow gentle at the same

16

time. In a marvellous sort of way it had you listening especially to him without losing the over-all balance of the band. Of course, it might have been just us, his family, who heard it; but I don't think so. You could tell by the way the others listened, leaving their drinks till he'd finished: he was something special to them too, all right. And like the rest of them, he had his favourite solo, something he'd do every time, which he'd written himself. 'You Can Have Your Cake and Eat It If You Try'. Something rag-time, up tempo, loud, and it stretched him for a high note at the end which everyone else except him thought he'd never make. But he did. Like a dream. And it always brought the house down.

But the odd Sunday wasn't enough. And that's how it happened. One night he went in through the foyer with a couple of friends and he left through the stage door with Freddie Flower and his All Stars. As sudden and unexpected as that. At breakfast time there was a note in his place instead of him. Pure Hollywood! Pure hell! I could never say for poor old Max because she went very close about it, but it was a knife in me that seemed to cut my whole life open: it changed my shape like a gutter's blade changes a fish into so much flesh and rubbish. We were left with the market licence, the stall, and the clothes he didn't want; an allowance which came by post; and the big question to answer of how, between the two of us, we'd failed to make up for what he'd lost.

Chapter Two

It's weird how you deal with a bad time. I remember seeing a woman being interviewed on the telly: she'd had three children taken off into care and was just going to be thrown out of her flat for not paying her rent. On top of that she was eight months gone. They filmed her sitting in a tatty chair holding her boy friend's hand and looking at him like he was Jesus.' I must say, you look happy,' the interviewer said. What a thing to say! But she smiled at her man and her face lit up, and she said, 'Yeah, we have our moments, don't we?' So it was a good thing to say, really illuminating. And I could see it. It's human nature to make something out of nothing, to clutch at clouds, because if we couldn't, the human race would've given up in disgust thousands of years ago. It wasn't totally surprising, then, that in the middle of all that aggravation with the Coxes – in fact, on the very night of the lights business – I was lifted up off my feet and bumped head over heels with pleasure. 'Are you happy?' someone could have said. Well, I certainly had my moment.

I didn't know her name at first, but she was at the Albion Supporters' Club disco. I'd gone there with Nick and a couple of the crowd, and we'd got up to do one of those novelty things where you all end up in a circle dancing with everyone else. There was a crowd of girls doing it, too, laughing and calling things out to one another – and at first I kidded myself I wasn't taking too much notice of any of them; but as the dance went on I found myself angling my body more and more to this one on my right. It happens sometimes. You're not looking anywhere special, you're concentrating on your feet, but somehow you sort of *know* someone's there, dancing the way you do; and here and there you start to move together, and then one of you smiles. I suppose I did: anyway, I know she did, and it gave me this tingle down my back that had me concentrating hard just to keep my feet moving. Very nice. And that might have been that – back to our places, no big deal, just a good experience – but before either of us knew what was happening, the lights went

18

all dim, the music got slower, the mirror ball was sparkling round the walls, and there we were with my hands on her waist and hers round my neck. It was as if I'd freaked out for a second or two, and suddenly there I was pressed up against her. It was untrue. I couldn't find the breath to say a word, and I daren't look round to see Nick's reaction, so I just stared at her and she stared at me and, God, I was *weightless*. If it never happens again, I thought, I'll remember this feeling for the rest of my life. It was perfection, and even thinking about it makes me want to put my head back and howl like a happy dog. Her waist moved very gently, warm and silky, and I kept a firm grip without squeezing, while my neck felt hot and cold at the same time. It was unbelievable. Neither of us said a thing, just swallowed, smiled a few times, and got to know each other's eyes. And then it was over. The music stopped, the lights went up, and she said, 'Thanks a lot,' as if all I'd done was sell her a new leather belt. She went one way and I went the other, tripping over my feet in a twist to find Nick, and that was that. She vanished like Cinderella and I drank a pint and a half of cider without knowing what I was doing.

Well, who gets to sleep after a thing like that? I went all round that bed in every possible position, paying for the pleasure I'd had with a weird new ache that wouldn't even tell me what it was, let alone go away. It wasn't pleasure any more, and it wasn't pain; the nearest I could get was a sort of mixture of pride and jealousy. Pride because I'd never even been looked at by a girl before; and jealousy of anyone who knew her well enough to call her by her name.

Max was up late glueing linings into half a dozen new handbags, and the squeak of the press and the smell of the glue were enough to keep anyone awake. But even she knew there was something up. It must have been one o'clock when she came in with a glass of lemon.

'What's up with you, Kev? Tossing and turning. You going over that lights business?'

I'd forgotten all about it. 'Yeah.'

'Don't let it get you down, love. They've shot their bolt there. See if I'm not right. Electrician's bound to find the silver paper; he'll know that can't be any accident.'

'Hope so.'

'He must do. Anyway, try and get off. Sunday tomorrow.'

'Yeah.' And a geography essay to write and no notes done yet.

'Want a tablet?'

'No thanks. I'm all right. Over-tired.' I looked at Max bending over me. The big bosom, the ruffled hair. But I didn't see her tired eyes. Instead, I saw the disco girl's, big and clear and blue. Had *she* got an essay to write? (Did she go to school, even?) Where did she live? And was she asleep yet, or was she pushing her legs around the bed like me?

'Kev, you got a pain? You look a bit flushed.'

'No, I'm all right.'

'You sure?'

'Yeah, why wouldn't I be?'

Max shrugged and went then, and I suddenly felt a sharp pang as I watched her, slightly hunched in her thin dressing gown but with a girl's feet, going back to her big, empty bed. This new mixed-up feeling I kept getting, where your heart races, thinking of someone special – she must have had it once, I thought: all up and down and inside out, but *alive*: with something secret to keep you going on the grind of everyday life. And it suddenly hit me that what I saw Max doing all the time was the total of what she was. Her leather and her stitching and my not getting to sleep was everything to her now. The lot. There wasn't anything else. No shuddering secret. And that seemed very sad to me.

You do go off to sleep in the end, of course. It takes you off with a touch you can't feel and fades away the thoughts you're trying to have. And then you're lost. Everything's out of your hands. Where you go for the night definitely isn't down to you: you mostly never know, just sometimes getting the faintest of clues when you wake back up. But that night I remember the Big Fellow was in the front of things, blowing his trumpet as large as life from the middle of Coxes' stall – which was marvellous while it lasted because it seemed as if he'd never gone away – and I was down there working the crowd for him collecting the money, moving about in the directions his trumpet told me, just the way Alfie Cox did for his father. 'And another over there, and another over there . . . ' but it was all said in the words of a trumpet's song. And then it ended, and I was awake, blinking in the light of an open door, choked at the Big Fellow fading away into his real life somewhere else. But suddenly hit by a great new high as I sat up and remembered like new what had happened the night before.

I'd laughed at girls, whistled after them, shouted things from the safety of a moving bus, but to actually dance with a girl the way I had was something else again. It was real magic, even worth letting go of my dream for. I kicked my legs in the bed and gave myself a hug round the neck just to remember how it felt.

'Kevin? If you want breakfast can you get it yourself? This rotten skiver's dried with a wrinkle.'

'O.K.' Sure! No trouble. I'd kill dragons today!

But you can't swing a sword and cut the head off a geography essay, especially when you're not too well prepared. So I soon came some of the way down to earth. I scribbled for a bit, really tried hard: but it was all crossing out and screwing up and a lot of swearing. I really couldn't concentrate; so in the end I left great gaps in the essay and decided to see what Reeve's Revision Notes there were in Smith's one night; and I did what had been lurking in the back of my mind all along. I waited till the leather punch was going loud and strong in Max's workroom, and I picked up the telephone and dialled.

'Is Nick there, please?'

'Hold on a minute.'

A clatter down, a pause, and then a clatter up.

'That you, Nick?'

'Yeah. Kev?'

'Yeah.'

'Wassup?'

'Nothing. You get home all right?'

'Yeah, why?'

'Just wondered. Good disco, wasn't it?'

'All right.'

'Hey – what about my luck, then?'

'What was that?'

'That girl.'

'Oh, her.'

'Good dancer, wasn't she?'

'Didn't notice, to be honest.'

'Yeah, good dancer. Never seen her before . . .'

'Haven't you? She gets down there sometimes.'

'Does she? Know her name?'

'No. Why?'

'No reason. You going next week?'

'Dunno. Doubt it. Sammy Wright's having a party. His mum's going away.'

'Oh, yeah. Not going, are you?'

'Probably. Anyhow, gotta ring off, we're just having our dinner.'

'Oh. Right. See you, then.'

'Yeah, see you . . .'

Click.

Jealous, that's all he was, I told myself. Funny bloke, Nick. If it'd been him with the girl I'd have had to be all enthusiastic; no doubt had to help in some scheme to find out her name and ask her out. But not the other way round. Some people are funny like that, even your good mates.

Sunday dragged on down from then. Day dreams don't get far when the other main character's called 'the girl'; and it was no good just making up a name for her; so the door seemed to shut on Saturday night, just a nice little dance at a disco and best forgotten.

By Tuesday, apart from a vague feeling *I* wouldn't be going to Sammy Wright's party, I'd put it all behind me. Which was just as well because what happened on Wednesday took such a savage grip on Max and me that every unnecessary thought was shaken out of us like so much loose change.

Our first sight of trouble was a thin back-sloping note from Simple Saunders, the market superintendent, folded small like a kid would in a big foolscap envelope. It was addressed to Mr W. M. Kendall. Would Mr Kendall oblige by writing for an appointment to see Mr Saunders by return?

It still got up Max's nose to be *Mr* Kendall. It grated on her that the council went on addressing her market receipts to the Big Fellow even though she corrected them every time. So we couldn't think it wasn't for her; in fact we both knew what it was all about – the fused lights in our standard.

'I'll do it by return all right! And it won't be one of those "many happy" ones, either. He won't know what's hit him. If that old idiot wants to charge me for the repair he's got a real fight coming!' She went out of the kitchen waving the letter like a flag, with that look in her eye which told the world Ms Max Marchant was ready to take anybody on, and win.

I left her to it and went to school. She'd sort it out and come back and do her impersonation of him at tea-time: picking his nose and bowing to the mayor. I didn't give it another thought till I heard the angry flap of that letter again when I walked in through the door.

'What the hell d'you think this was all about?' she shouted at me, as if I was to blame in some peculiar way. Sometimes she made it very hard to be on her side.

'I dunno. Wasn't it the lights?'

'No, it wasn't the lights. I didn't get round to even say the word "lights".'

'I don't know, then.' I threw down my books and made for the tea-pot.

'It's the licence. Only the blasted licence!'

The tea-pot was stone cold: normally she lived out of it like sheriffs do out of coffee jugs.

'We're paid up, aren't we? Month in advance? You've got receipts.'

'Oh, yes! There's never any hassle about taking our money!' She was charging up and down, bumping into furniture, a hand in her hair. 'It's the licence itself. Did you know it runs out at the end of the month?'

'No, not exactly. But it runs out every year sometime about now. They just bung up the rent and re-issue.'

'Right. Well today it was different.' She watched me filling the kettle. 'Listen to this, if you can believe it.' She was shaking. 'God, I need something stronger.' Her tough leather-worker's hands trembled as she poured herself a Bacardi and Coke, without much Coke. 'My licence was taken out by . . . your

23

father . . . three years ago, right? When he came out? We went along and he signed the papers. Yes?'

I kept nodding. Waving her glass, all her body moving except her eyes, fixing me with the anger she'd got for Saunders, quivering on the verge – I knew if I dared to take my eyes off her she'd throw the glass at my head. I'd never seen her in such a rage, not even when the Big Fellow went.

'So!' A gulp for breath; but it was all Bacardi. 'If I want to renew this year I've got to have it signed by the original licensee . . . by your precious father. How about that?' She threw the crumpled letter on the table and shook her free hand jerkily in the loose curls of her hair. 'Eh? How about that for a clever little trick? Eh?'

The water was pouring out of the top of the kettle. I reckoned I could turn it off while I spoke. 'But they can't get away with that these days. It's against the sex what's-it act. They haven't got a leg to stand on.'

'Oh, haven't they? Let me tell you, they're cleverer than that.' She was fighting for breath now. 'Listen . . . for the past three years . . . they've renewed automatically – so Saunders says – only because no one else has put in for our pitch. Now Cox has wised up to our situation – and he's applied.' She downed the last of her drink and thumped the glass on to the table, leaning on it. 'And that means we can't automatically renew. Not me, anyhow. *I'm a new applicant.* The bastards!'

She poured some more Bacardi, and I got the kettle on.

'You mean, if Dad does it he gets it automat . . . ?'

'Not guaranteed: but as sitting tenant, a good payer, never any hassle, they must favour him. Odds on he'd get it, Saunders says. They usually do. But he could hardly keep the smile off his face while he told me. That creep knows our position, that I'm not the official licensee. And now Cox knows it, too. No one'll be applying from our family but me. And if I apply I'm only the same as him – a new applicant for that pitch.' She took a good mouthful. 'With him and Saunders hand in glove you don't need ten guesses to know which way the nod'll go.'

'Christ! So Cox could've pulled this stunt before?'

'If he'd thought of it.'

'Well, then . . . ' I stared at her. Couldn't she see it? It was quite clear to me, perfectly straightforward, very obvious: just a simple business matter. It wouldn't be pleading, there'd be no grovelling in just asking . . .

'Don't you even think it, Kevin. I wouldn't ask that man to pull me out of quicksand.'

She gulped at her drink again and started smacking her hand against the wall behind her.

I quickly switched the kettle off, before it could start screaming into such a dangerous atmosphere.

Like a slow-growing cancer it had taken nearly two years to show itself, then all of a sudden it was critical. Not since the day he first went had there been a word said against him. The two of us had been like one of those families who won't talk politics or religion because it only uncovers bad feeling. Some people would rather keep the bandages on, the screens round, and we'd quietly decided to be like that. All right, when he'd gone that first morning leaving the note behind there'd been plenty of tears and bitter shouts: but they'd been into the air, and there'd been no hatred of him spoken between us: only some sort of angry pity for ourselves: all at once we were all each other had, and there was no point risking any sharp spikes in our knot. He'd gone, and we'd been left to wonder why we'd come second-best to his music: but neither of us had led a closing of the ranks against him. It goes without saying I'd always wondered what she'd do if he ever wrote asking to come back – or if he ever came bowling in one day, all guilty grin and trumpet case – but we never talked about it. So her blow-up and her grab for the bottle was a shock; and no shock at all; and with a glass of milk and the excuse of a load of homework I threw myself down on my bed to think.

All right, I told myself, he'd done the dirty and gone, and his 'nothing to do with *us*, Max' in the letter might or mightn't be true – there was no way I could know. But that wasn't the point. What I couldn't see was how she couldn't use him. After all, he owed us a hell of a big favour, and where was the weakness in taking him up on that? I couldn't see any real difference at all between calmly cashing the monthly cheque he always had sent and getting his signature on the licence application. Max was just being stubborn, cutting off her nose to spite her face. All she had to do was make a few simple enquiries, find out where he was, and send the papers to him. He'd do what she wanted, as good as gold, we both knew that.

But she *was* stubborn; and independent. And, OK, I could see that side, too. Why should a successful working woman have to depend on a runaway husband for the right to make a living? But if that was the way things were, well . . .

I stared at the ceiling and slid the Hohner mouth organ the Big Fellow had given me out from under the pillow. I warmed it, got the shiny tin to the temperature of my hands, and put it to my lips. Quietly, gently, I tongued the bitter wooden reeds and blew down into them. Hollow cheeked, closing my eyes, I sucked and blew as if the Hohner was an egg and the music something fragile. I started a slow foot tap to 'Worried Man Blues' and gradually I began to fly away.

It was a real comfort, that mouth organ. I got a kick out of the quiet sense of power making your own music always seems to give: I got a kick out of the feeling of performing like the Big Fellow, even in the privacy of my bedroom, taking chances with notes and variations on a tune as if a big audience was listening: but most special of all, and deeply secret, I never played without thinking about him – wherever he was – and thinking how proud of me he'd be if he could hear. Especially in the dark, I thought like that; in the light, when Max was around, I wouldn't even let him into my head.

But that night I couldn't play for long. Because as soon as I thought about the Big Fellow, and Max not wanting to ask him a favour, the most selfish, shaming thought came muscling into my mind. I was *glad* about the letter; and glad about the decision Max had made. Lose the licence and what would there be? No more Alfie Cox to worry about, that's what! Throw it all in, live off the army pension and the supplementary and the only worries I'd have in my life would be essays I hadn't done, and was that girl going to be at the disco on Saturday?

And that'd suit me fine, to be honest.

So wasn't I the biggest creep on God's earth for thinking it? Lying there I started to feel as if I'd done the running away from

Max myself: or at least from the aggravation her business stood for: and the bitter reeds suddenly tasted acid enough to spit them away from my mouth.

Chapter Three

Some people live for a fight, they're driven on by aggravation. Like politicians. They seem to go round looking for some small war they can win in the way rangy dogs run from one side of the road to the other to see off the autumn leaves. You hear it all the time. 'Wait till I get hold of him!' coming from people who'd much sooner bear a grudge than one of those olive branches. But that's not me. Not Kevin Kendall. I hate conflict. I'll compromise, decide not to take things up, suddenly go deaf rather than look for some argument. I'm one of those who'd always settle out of court if I could. Which is why all my Saturdays were hell; and why I looked forward to the Saturday after the licence letter like you look forward to toothache. It was going to be painful as hell. If I could only keep Max away things might be all right: on my own I could just about cope. But once she saw the Coxes she'd be out to wind things up, and there'd be a real screaming match out there.

Getting out of bed I felt the floor shake under me like a walk-way at the fair. The light switch had moved somewhere else on the wall, and in the kitchen I tried to boil an empty kettle. Down inside, my bowels rolled around with nerves, and the thought of food – even the sight of a slice – bloated me up. I was in a state before I got anywhere, and some serious illness would have been a small price to pay for keeping me away.

Max hadn't woken up when I went out. I wondered if she'd taken a tablet to help her sleep. She had a few for when she got all tense, and I reckoned this might be the time for it. Good job, then, I thought – her Mogadon would last her well into the morning, dampen her down – and any help, even pills, was going to be handy.

I knew what we were up against. Market people, real market people, are as cocky as cabbies. They reckon never to be bested, they're natural winners. Shouting the odds the way they do, you can take it they mean it. You have to be confident to shout that loud – just listen to the embarrassment of someone's father at a school fête in comparison. Well, we were up against not only the Coxes but the whole of that tradition, and did I feel it that morning! I was an outsider, a Saturday brat, and I walked down their lines with this huge feeling of envy for all their family experience. A charity stall, ours was, compared to all theirs, and I'd never felt it digging in more sharply.

Just a word would have made all the difference. Something easy, like 'Morning, Kev,' as I pulled the stall along the High Pavement. Just a little inch of belonging showing somewhere. But it didn't happen, and I was still a kid on my own as I set up the stall in the half light.

In their clever new way the Coxes were acting as good as gold. They were ahead of me, but keeping to their own space as if ours was radio-active. Alfie Cox was so well-behaved he could have been doing the Duke of Edinburgh's Award. And, of course, the lights worked. The plug went in sweetly and the bulbs flashed on full and bright – a sure signal that the Coxes had upped the stakes this week.

If only it could stay like that while something got sorted out. If only Max could stop herself from rising to them . . .

We set-up properly after a breakfast which neither of us touched. And she *had* taken a tablet. I knew the signs: they affected her more than most people. She moved a bit more slowly, yawned a lot, handled the tissue round her handbags as if it was folded lead, and when we'd unloaded she lowered the empty boxes under the stall like baby coffins. If she looked at either of the enemy I didn't see her – and for an hour I really started to think that things would be all right. We'd do what fighting and manoeuvring had to be done in the proper place, and we'd get through Saturday without a show up.

So it seems ridiculous that it was me who set it all off. Me – and the girl from the disco.

Perhaps I was drugged as well by then. With things seeming to go smoothly perhaps I'd relaxed, because certain other private thoughts were finding room to roam around. Would *she* be at the disco that night? Was there any chance of a dance like the last one? Could I work up the bottle to ask her out some time? Standing there between sales, re-hanging the belts, stuffing tissue into handbags to fill them out, I mouthed my questions and heard her answers, and I even began to see her. I saw her reflected in the shop windows and in the dazzle of the lights. It's crazy what that sort of fantasy does to you.

And was it real or imagination when I saw her pushing past the back of Cox's crowd? I didn't know for sure – and either way I couldn't believe it.

She wasn't the first I saw. I had a warning, like the click before the phone rings. I recognized one of her friends, a face from that crowd of dancers, one I couldn't mistake with big, staring eyes. And I nearly dropped the shoulder bag I was stuffing as I saw who was with her. Coming through, all serene, her head up, her hair shining; coming through towards me, making some smiling remark about Charlie Cox doing his stuff. It was admiring, a chuck of her head, a blink of her eyes, and something said quietly to her friend. And then she stopped sidling past, and a terrible jealous stab twisted round inside as I saw who had grabbed her attention. Alfie – out in the crowd collecting, who'd leant an arm across in front of her and was saying something to make her smile. *My* smile. The smile I'd gone home grinning about: and seeing it given to him gave me a whole new pain I never want to feel again.

Up in front of the crowd Charlie Cox turned his back to pick up something else, and God knows what came over me, but before I knew what I was doing I was up on my feet on a stool and lifting the flap of the shoulder bag I had in my hand.

'Here you are, over here, ladies and gents!' I suddenly heard myself shouting. 'A shoulder bag for all occasions. Just look at it, hand-made locally in finest leather. Lined with the softest of silk. A nice present for anyone who likes good things.' I threw out the tissue as if it was fivers and ran my hand over the lining.

'*Kevin!*' I heard from Max. 'You bloody *mad*?!' But half of Cox's crowd had turned their heads to look at me, with those blank bewildered looks people have before they realize what they're seeing is a fight.

I raked the crowd with my eyes for the top of the girl's head as I drew in a deep breath to take her attention off Alfie some more. But I couldn't see her; she must have moved on: and old man Cox had used that couple of seconds' silence to start thumping his box with his stick.

'Well, 'ow d'you like that, then? Competition from the bloody kids! Marvellous, i'n it? Who tipped up your cradle, Baby Bunting?'

They laughed, the way you do at a sarcastic teacher, and their faces started turning from one to the other of us. And suddenly the one thing I wanted to do was to get down. I wanted to be a million miles away. But I had to fight back. I'd started it, I had to win through for my own self respect, let alone for the sake of keeping Alfie off that girl.

'It's a unique bag, this. That's right, *unique*. Hand-made here in Thames Reach, no two exactly alike. You can feel the smoothness, smell the real leather. This is none of your plastic muck!' I flung out a hand in the direction of Charlie Cox and his second-rate rubbish.

He laughed, a really loud roar like actors and vicars can do, and he hit his box again. 'Oh dear, oh dear,' he said. 'Nasty! Vinegar in the gripe water?'

'Get down for crissake!' Max was hissing, pulling at me; and the shoulder bag slipped out of my hand.

'Come on, then, cocker,' Cox shouted. 'Tell 'em all about my rubbish. Listen 'ard, girls, I might want a witness!' He waved his stick over the crowd for quiet, and he folded his arms.

But my mouth had gone as dry as dust, and Max had got her foot firm on the shoulder bag. I couldn't think of a single word to say. To go on with my leather versus plastic 'rubbish' talk would get us up in court and out of the market quicker than any trick of his. And I'd run dry on the attractions of the shoulder bag, even if I could've got it back in my hands. All I wanted to do was get down and stay down. Then perhaps buy a knife to slit my throat. But meanwhile I stood there with my mouth open, as awkward as a heckler when the hall goes all quiet.

And Charlie Cox wasn't going to let me off the hook.

'Come on, son, don't be a teaser. We all know teasers, don't we, girls? There's nothing worse, is there?'

I willed myself. I prayed to God. If ever there was a moment for my brilliant reply, this was it. A line to cap his. A devastating come-back to get a big laugh against him and a round of applause for me.

But nothing came.

'Aaaaa!' said Cox in a sympathetic voice. 'He's shot his bolt. An' we know all about that an' all, don' we? Well, don't say I don't give youth a chance. You come back when your voice breaks, Sunshine!'

I got down, got out of sight by pretending to grab for the bag on the ground and crouched there where I was. The bastard! He'd shown me up rotten without looking like a bully. He'd given me every chance to go on, and I hadn't been up to it.

I looked up. There were a few friendly clucks for me, but his crowd had turned back to him: and with a master stroke he was holding up a good leather briefcase. 'Rubbish?' he was saying. '*Rubbish*? Now 'ere's a leather bargain even our young friend'd like to get 'is 'ands on . . .'

They laughed: and I stared into the angry mask of Max's face.

'You bloody fool!' she hissed. 'What stupid game d'you think you're playing?'

My neck pulsed and the feel of grit pricked my eyes. I re-stuffed the bag with tissue and kept a bit back for blowing my nose.

'When I want *that* sort of help I'll tell you!'

I turned my back. It goes without saying, the girl had gone. And I was left feeling like a kid who's said 'knickers' to the lady next door and been given a good hiding in the street. Six years old, I felt. Because six years old I'd acted. And the only thing that kept me from jumping off the ferry was the thought of seeing the girl that night.

By seven o'clock I was heading through the estates to the Thames Reach Albion Supporters' Club. Better than balls for bouncing back, people like me are. And if I didn't have a good reason for trying to rebound tonight, I'd never have one. I needed to see that girl like you need water in a marathon.

Nick's dad was the member who got us in, and he used the place like a pub. It was as depressing as the rest of the third division outfit from the street – corrugated roof, patched-up windows, chipped enamel signs about guard dogs – but inside, the long curtains and the concealed lighting really made you think of a good night out; and that's what Nick and I went for, when his dad would take us. The special teenage discos were supposed to be good money spinners so they had quite a few – and didn't the club need money! Low down in the third, working off a League fine for bad behaviour, hooligan supporters banned from away games, Thames Reach Albion needed every penny it could get. Once every so often membership cards were checked to keep the hoorays out, and without Nick and his dad I could always be turned away. But I'd risked it once or twice on my own, and that Saturday night I reckoned it was well worth taking a chance again.

Being me, of course, I worried about it, all the way through one of those careful shaves I have once a week; but I got in all right: the secretary walked right past me in the entrance hall and even called me 'Kev'.

I bought myself a cider and sat down in a corner, waiting in the darkness as tense as a cat in the bushes. But it was early yet – I'd been miles too eager to get there – so I took my drink slowly and let the tingle wear off. I sat and took an interest in watching Johnnie Dark the DJ set himself up; at first because there was nothing better to do and it took my mind off the waiting, but in the end because he got me hooked. I really admire professionals. I've got a lot of time for them. Johnnie Dark didn't mess around, showing off to the kids, the big DJ. He didn't talk to anyone, didn't drink, just gave every ounce of his attention to what he was doing: plugging in his lights and oil-slides, listening to his turntables through a telephone, adjusting his speakers, arranging his records; he had a quick-fingered routine, and he worked fast. It was like I tried to be when I was putting up the stall, not a wasted movement, and not satisfied till it was right. But he was miles better. And you could tell that just now he might be scowling, intent on his equipment to get it right; but in a minute he'd be switching up the volume, turning on the personality, and making everyone think his show just happened the way it came out. Everything would seem to fall to hand – but only because he'd worked hard to get it that way. I enjoyed watching him; and I was fascinated because he put me in mind of someone.

For a time I couldn't work out who it was: and then it came to me. It was Charlie Cox. Charlie was like that: everything ready, props to hand, nothing left to chance: then, start the routine, and everything coming out sounding as if he'd just made it up. Week after week I listened to him, got to know his tricks, and still he had me watching with my mouth open.

Till today! A gulp of cider went down the wrong way. Christ, how could I forget, even for a minute? *What about today?* What about that show up? I shook my head to try to get rid of the thought. What sort of stupid need to impress had got me up to mix it with him? I went cold at the thought of it. The *embarrassment*. I'd given myself a present that morning of a moment I wouldn't forget as long as I lived. I'd never lose the look on Cox's face, and I'd see those market expressions in my nightmares for ever, every one of the grins they'd turned on me. And Max! What about her shrieking anger at the stupid wrong-foot move I'd made?

I drowned the thought with a giant gulp, one of those really big ones your mouth can hardly cope with but you daren't spit back. I tried to think of something else. And as luck would have it the first thump of the disco suddenly bounced back off the walls and deadened all thought. I sat up and slid my glass away. A fair old crowd had gathered, the bar was busy, and there was a definite feel of pleasure in the air. The only question was, was I going to be part of it or not?

She wasn't there yet. There was a big gang of boys on their own, aertex, white boots and eyes all round for mates; an older lot in pairs, careful hair, all image; and a crowd of girls like the one *she'd* been with before. But there was no sign of her, and no sign of any special face she might have come with.

I think I knew right then that she wasn't coming. I chucked the thought out, naturally, gave it the Big Ben treatment, telling myself it was like at a football match where it's always possible to score in the minute before time: but I couldn't shake the nagging thought that that was only when the result didn't matter; and for me that night mattered like nobody's business.

And I was right the first time. She didn't come. The records played, Johnnie Dark did well, and after an hour he knew for him and I knew for me that the shape of the evening had been set.

The second cider hardly lasted ten minutes, and the third was the swift drink of someone with a throat to clear.

34

I went to the gents. It was on my way out. I'd go home and finish off the evening with Max, I thought – which I ought to do more often, anyway. Poor old Max. She never made any bones of it, but every Saturday night was like this for her. My last thought in that darkness was for me, though. As I dived out through the dusty curtain I suddenly wondered if the girl and her crowd could all be at the party Nick had gone to. Oh, God! How about that for a superior look on his face Monday morning?

I stood at the urinal – and then the biggest humiliation of all! A couple of older men were washing their hands and talking by the air-blow; they wouldn't move away; and as I felt their stares on my back, I froze. I was dying to go: I'd got three pints inside me: and could I coax a start? They'd dropped their voices, they *had* to know I was in all sorts, and the harder I tried the more I was wasting my time. So what did you do when that happened? Make a loud joke and clear off? Count the tiles, compute the thirteen times table, work out how many slits in the drain covers there'd be along the line of nine stalls? I tried desperately to think of anything but the job in hand – but still nothing happened.

I gave up with a small pantomime of shake and zip. But there was no way of disguising it was another show-up. Sometime I'd have to make a note of the date of this terrible day.

I had to face it out, though. I'd go over and wash my hands: let them think they were wrong.

'No luck, then, mate?'

I grinned, and knew what a stupid look I must have on my face. 'No. Just a try. I'm off now.'

They grinned, too, but there was a certain sympathy.

'Still, needn't be a waste o' time. Want a bargain? Want the last one?' A fat guy with a fist full of notes and *Funk* on his sweatshirt was holding out a long jewellers' box.

I shook my head. 'What is it?'

He handed me the box. 'Have a look: but don't be all night.' A sense of conspiracy suddenly hung in the air, strong as the disinfectant blocks.

The box snapped open with a jump in my hand.

'That's nice.'

It was a ladies' watch, gold – or gold looking – with a matching bracelet, a white face, smart Roman numbers, and thin black hands ticking away in quartz. *Geneva*, it was called.

'Yeah, 'tis nice, isn't it? I only had a few. The strap's worth what I'm asking.'

It was certainly a good-looking watch, plain and expensive, what Max would call good taste: the sort of watch she'd wear. But it had to be a tenner, even on the cheap like this.

'Give us a quid.'

'Eh?'

'Give us a quid. Look, fully guaranteed.' He lifted out the folded card from the box in my hand. 'A twelvemonth.'

I was very tempted. My hand had gone straight to my pocket. After all, I had a bit of money to spend now, and wouldn't something like this give old Max a lift after what I'd done to-day?

But there was one more question to ask.

'Where'd it come from?'

The fat man groaned and took the box off me. 'Oh, come on, son. You don't ask silly questions like that when you're getting a bargain. "*Where'd it come from?*" A quid for a gold watch? Where'd you think?' He laughed to the others and put the box into his trouser pocket.

But seeing the box go away again suddenly got me: that, and the feeling that I needed to walk away with something out of this disaster of an evening when even a pee had been too much for me.

'Hold on, I'll have it.' The pound was out of my pocket and into his hand, the box out of his pocket and into mine in less than five of those thin quartz ticks.

'You've done yourself a favour, son.'

He went quickly, and the others with him. I rearranged my pocket, pushed the box down deep, under my hankie, just in case I got stopped on the way home. I was pleased with it, I think I actually smiled. Now Max'd have something to wear in place of that red digital which spent its life dangling from a cup hook in the kitchen because the Big Fellow had given it to her. And she had a birthday coming up, didn't she? She'd be happy to take it from me on her birthday, when there was some excuse: but the present would be for today, really, for all that embarrassment I'd given her.

On my own, I went back to the urinal and let go. No problem. But no girl, I told the wall; definitely a disappointment there; although I had something in my pocket to bring a smile to Max's face, and that was something not to be sneezed at.

Chapter Four

Indoors, though, I walked smack into a row. Even as it hit me I tried to think what had caused it all of a sudden: after all, we'd seen each other since the market show-up. Was it a rotten programme on the telly, giving her time to brood; or too much Bacardi; or the wrong time of the month? All the blame on her, of course. But I'd had a drink, too, and I had my own disappointment to swallow, so I could well have slammed the front door too hard.

She came at me sideways.

'You done your homework this week?'

'Yes!' I stopped in the doorway. I'd been ready to come in and sit next to her, put an arm round her: not a thing I did often – didn't she know how lucky she'd nearly been?

'Proper homework? A bit of French, some maths, some physics? Not just fiddling about with what you like?'

'Oh – aren't I supposed to like some of it?'

'You know what I mean. A little bit of getting down to it, boy.' She wouldn't look at me; just sat staring angrily at the row of green lights on the stereo, her mouth turned down and two ugly lines running from her nose to her chin which only came out at times like this.

I must have sighed, because she suddenly twisted in her seat and looked at me with blazing eyes, a fierceness on her face she wouldn't use on Cox – that sudden sort of hatred which is strictly reserved for family.

'Well I'll tell you, unless you want to end up like your father with sweet f. a. behind you, you're going to knuckle down and get your exams, Kevin Kendall. Get yourself qualified at *something*. That market stall's not supposed to be giving you ideas. We don't need a Charlie Cox in the family, thank you very much . . . '

So that was it. She was squeezing out the poison that had been festering. One of my guesses had been right: I'd been stupid to think it had been passed over as best forgotten.

'I didn't do it for that. I don't want to be like Charlie Cox . . .'

'So why, then? What the hell made you suddenly act the goat this morning?'

'I'd have thought that was obvious!' I threw it back at her, but I was only saying words, playing for time, racking my brains for the right lie: because I couldn't share the embarrassment of the truth about the girl going past. The lie came. 'I just wanted Cox to see he's got a fight on his hands. Telling him we're not taking it lying down. Cox doesn't have sole right to stand up and shout the odds in that market.'

'Well, don't you ever dare do it again. You're not cut out for it, so don't start thinking you are. You're not bumming round in this life without a proper job, not able to handle a bit of freedom . . .'

I shifted my weight. Her face was staring away from me again. She was going off at the Big Fellow, really: but that was no reason for having a go at me.

'Do you want another drink?'

She flashed round again, half-rose over the back of her chair and threw a shaking finger at me. 'Don't be bloody saucy!' she shouted. The movement altered her weight in the chair and a leg kicked out, sending the glass on the floor cracking against the bottle she'd got out of sight. 'Go and get down to some work!'

This time I made sure to close the door quietly and went into my bedroom. The desk top was still littered with going out, the tube of spot disguiser, the after-shave, a dirty hankie. Christ, coming back after that failure was a bad enough business as it was, without all Max's aggravation! Feeling finished, I sat on the bed to untie my boots – and dug myself hard in the side with her birthday watch.

I couldn't bear to look at it again, not now. All the pleasure had gone out of it. I put it in an old shoe in the wardrobe.

I tidied up the desk and slid a few books about. It was annoying, but she was dead right. I'd put off doing the geography essay till I'd got the Reeve's Notes, but in over a week I'd done nothing about buying them.

And she was wrong, too. I might have had a sneaking admiration for the man, but I'd never seen me being another

39

Charlie Cox when I grew up. I liked the way he lived off his wits, but there was no way I could tell if living off my wits was me. Any more than I could tell if I could stand up on my own like the Big Fellow had done. Living off his talent while it paid, doing the only thing he knew: following his star.

And destroying Max to do it.

I shut all my books and sat up straight. Because that's what he'd done all right, and it was a hell of a rotten thought to come crowding in right now. I'd been too close to it to see it – no, to *admit* it. I'd felt sorry for her the way you do, but just as sorry for myself; now, in the middle of feeling sore at what she'd said, I had to own up to knowing that my choices were a hell of a lot better than hers. All right, she ran her little business, but the way she made those few extra bob was all there was to her now. She deserved to be doing much more with herself than that. That other Max had gone, the slim one, the one who could be crazy, wrestle you, take off the major behind his back – the one who could *laugh*. The Big Fellow had run off with her as well as his trumpet.

I got into bed. Another Saturday night with me all mixed up again. But the girl had gone: I wouldn't kick around the bed thinking of her tonight: there was more serious family business to sort this week. Max might have wound me up, but she was the one who mattered. I'd got to see she kept the little bit of life she'd got left, at the very least. Because otherwise things didn't look too bright. If she lost the market stall, where the hell would she turn? To the Bacardi she'd had down by her side? Suddenly, that didn't seem all that unlikely. All of which meant that if I really wanted to help, there was no way round it – *somehow I'd got to take on Charlie Cox*. I'd got to find some lever to make him pull out of wanting our space – and fast, by the looks of it, before the depression Max was going into really took her down. But it was a killer thought, that, and it kept me awake a lot longer than the girl had managed to do.

I'd made my own mind up on what I needed to do for Max, something I usually did. In fact, it wasn't often that I wanted someone to tell me how to think: but on that geography homework I certainly needed a few potted thoughts. Reading a pile of long books with all the wisdom of the examiners would have been the right way, but even the school didn't expect that, not for 'mocks', and Reeve's Notes sounded just about right.

On the Monday night I called into Smith's after drama to get some; a quick nip in on my way home, my mind miles away from any problems except my geography. Even my wish to see the girl again, strong as it had been while it lasted, had faded into the mists. So I didn't know whether to cheer or groan when I saw who was sitting at the till on the upstairs book section. Not that I had any choice over what happened to me. Sherbert seemed to explode inside me and my legs went like two daisy stalks. It was *her* – the girl – sitting on her stool and sliding a couple of paperbacks into one of their bags. I honestly reckon if I could have trusted my legs not to tip me over I would have turned round on my heel and walked straight out; but I couldn't, so I kept on going, didn't break step. I swore, and I did somersaults and cartwheels and jumped off the top board: but I didn't break step. I just had to make it to the cover of the bookshelves, that was all.

But she saw me. She looked up from the customer she'd just served to stare into space the way they do, and she saw me. Caught as in kipper! She almost frowned, but not quite. She almost opened her eyes wide, but they only flickered. She definitely kept control of her expression – and then decided to let go of her smile.

It was like the sun coming out.

I stopped and dropped a shoulder. 'Hi!' I said, and cursed inside. What did I think I was, some cowboy?

'Hello.'

I walked over to her, as cool as I could. 'Oh, do you work here, then?'

'No, I'm down a coal mine.' We both laughed, her for real. 'I'm still at school, aren't I?'

I scratched my head like a hick: felt myself doing it and couldn't stop my hand in time. It was all going wrong. I was casting myself as the pigeon-toed idiot in this set up.

'I just do a bit of part-time, two nights and Saturdays . . .'

She served a customer, automatically, still giving her attention to me.

It was my turn to say something. 'Oh, it's just, I thought I saw you, Saturday. Along the High Pavement.'

'Could be. We do have half-hour for dinner. Generous, isn't it?' She made a face, eyes to heaven, very pretty. The Kendall heart was thumping. 'Where were you? I never saw you. You never spoke, did you?'

Didn't I just! But thank God she hadn't seen the show-up. 'Oh, I help on one of the stalls. I couldn't leave it, that was all. You'd gone before I could give you a shout.'

'Oh.' She served someone else, then she looked up and gave me a Monday version of that Saturday night look. 'I suppose you could say we're in the same line of business, then.'

'Yeah, I s'pose you could.'

Her face changed. It closed up, suddenly went official again. 'Everything all right, Wendy?'

I should have smelt her. An old lavender supervisor had crept up behind me; and her polite enquiry really meant stop talking to this boy and get on with your job.

'Yes, thanks, Mrs B.'

But 'Wendy', she'd said! So that was her name. *Wendy*. I liked it. Looked forward to saying it – not that I'd be saying anything just yet with Old Lavender hovering. I wandered away to look at the Reeve's Notes: did well, pretended not to see her daggers look from over Wendy's shoulder.

And Old Lavender was in for a surprise, too, because I wasn't just a hanger-on the way she thought I was: I was genuinely going to buy something. And there was the book I wanted. *Reeve's Examination Revision Notes on Physical Geography*. But I wouldn't be in too much of a hurry. If I could hang about till the old girl lost interest I might have a quick chance for one more word with Wendy.

A girl of around ten was standing near me, looking at the paperbacks, looking for something special, you could tell by the way she was running her finger along the spines. Over the top Old Lavender was still standing by the till, showing Wendy how to ring up a book token, or something. I saw my chance.

'You looking for something special?' I asked the girl.

She gave me a look as if I'd said something filthy. I hadn't thought of that! Hell, I'd be thrown out of here on my ear if I wasn't careful, talking to strange girls.

'Ask the lady,' I said, quickly. 'Go on, don't be shy – she'll help you. That's what she's there for.'

The girl went on looking at me as if I was something nasty from under an old bit of lino. I moved away sharply.

But it worked. When I looked up again the girl was by the till talking to Old Lavender, and a couple of seconds later Old Lavender was bossing her way across the carpet towards the Puffins.

Quick as a flash, I made my move. Gliding round the tin globes like *Holiday on Ice*, the right money out on my palm, I slid up to Wendy and tipped the coins on to the check-out.

'This, please – and, er – do you ever go to the pictures?'

I stared at her blank face. She did it really well.

'That's ninety-five pence. See you outside at six. Thank you very much.' The *Reeve's Notes* went into the bag, the till was rung, and she was leaning over to serve the Puffin girl without giving me a second look.

Old Lavender watched me go – I could feel her eye-balls down the stairs – and I hurried out to the street. Well, the best of luck to her, I thought. She'd forced me into being bold, and see what had happened! I'd made the next move without stopping to think about it. Now all I regretted was not waiting for a proper shower after drama, and not making sure about my hair. But it was dark, I thought, and she'd seen me now, anyhow. And I wouldn't have to be long. Just ask her out and then get home to Max.

I walked the whole length of Hudson Street while I waited, down to the river on one side and then back on the other. It was busy on both pavements with tight-faced people: pushing on to buses, running in and out of closing doors, dodging the traffic. All rushing about their business, and no one else in the whole world with the special feeling I had inside! I was sorry for all of them, but much too pleased with myself to let it make me sad. *They* weren't meeting Wendy in twenty minutes. *They* weren't on the edge of something big and new. For all of them this was just the end of another rotten day. But for me, grotty old Thames Reach was a magic place tonight.

I looked hard at myself in a shop window. I turned up my duffel collar, a bit more Humphrey Bogart. I pulled my jeans bottoms a bit closer to my boots. All right, that'd have to do.

Now, the question was, what was I going to ask her out *to*? Like an idiot, that was something I hadn't thought through. Well, what was on at the pictures I'd so casually thrown in? I didn't have the first idea what the Regal was showing. It could easily be something totally out of keeping – some Walt Disney about a lost puppy, or a sex film, giving all the wrong ideas. They'd both be equally embarrassing. And there was nowhere else around here, except the Empress.

Except the Empress! That was a thought! I hadn't set foot in that place since the Big Fellow had disappeared through the stage door eighteen months before. Going in there hadn't seemed any more of a good idea than going back to the scene of an accident. But Nick reckoned some good groups got down there mid-week. And Wendy seemed to like music.

Well, I'd just have to play it by ear: busk along till the right tune came out.

I was back outside Smith's by now. A couple of dark cars with men in them were waiting for people to come out, and a big gorilla shape in a sheepskin coat was leaning in the doorway. I looked at him carefully. What an embarrassment if we were both waiting for the same girl . . .

The manager stood inside the door rattling his keys, letting out the staff in ones and twos as if it was eight a.m. at Holloway. 'Goodnight, Miss Clark. 'Night, Mrs B . . . '

I turned my face away. The dreaded Mrs B! Old Lavender. I didn't see why she should see the end of the story. If she saw me waiting here she'd soon boot me out if I shot in to see Wendy again. If ever I did . . . I pulled a face, out there in the open. Who knew what was going to happen? Like with a lot of things, you could only wait and see.

She came out. Third. She'd not hung about, then. That was a good sign, anyway.

'Goodnight, Wendy.'

''Night.'

She hadn't changed her mind, either. She didn't scurry off

like the others. Once she was out of the door she started looking about – and I shot my hand out of my pocket and waved like a politician. God, why couldn't I be myself?

'Hello,' she said. 'Listen, I haven't got long. My dad meets me at five past . . . '

We both turned round to look at the cars in the kerb. Just as if I'd have known which car was his!

'No, I haven't got to be too late, neither.'

'Well, then . . . '

Now we looked at one another, close together, near enough to share our breath, collars up, her face in a soft surround of curls and coat. It would have been great to kiss her.

I suddenly decided not to chance the pictures. 'I don't know what's on at the Empress. There's usually something. How you fixed for Wednesday?'

'OK.' She nodded seriously.

'Seven o'clock outside?'

'OK. But be there. My dad'll drop me off: but he won't leave me on my own.'

'Right. OK, then.'

'Right.'

She could have been laughing at me a bit, or at the situation. I wasn't sure. All I knew was we'd suddenly run out of words, just standing there staring at one another . . . and there definitely wasn't the time to get down to the real business of getting to know each other.

But there was one thing. 'By the way, I'm Kevin.'

'Evening, Kevin.' She did have a terrific sense of humour. 'I'm Wendy.'

'I know.'

'Thought you did. Should've seen your face when Mrs B said it.'

'Oh, yeah?' I gave her a grin, a caught-me-there look, but suddenly I wished her father would come. I wanted to get away, to work it out, get prepared for talking to her. It was stupid little moments like this when you gave all the wrong impressions. What I needed now was a brilliant, witty line to leave her laughing over, telling her what fun it was going to be, going out with me: instead of which all I could feel myself doing was hunching my shoulders and turning into that second-hand cowboy who said 'Hi!'

'Oh, there he is . . .'

'Ah – '

'You sound pleased!'

The face she pulled was shocked: pretend shocked: and I liked that, too.

'No, 'course not. But . . . ' John Wayne was telling the blacksmith's daughter he had to go off with the posse.

'Anyway, see you, Kevin.'

'Yeah, see you, Wendy. Wednesday.'

She ran to the car, a steel-grey Datsun with the door opened for her from inside. She turned and waved at me. Not shy.

I waved back, a big, confident one. I'd see her when I'd done for the outlaws. But it suddenly struck me that I was waving as much for her invisible father as I was for her. I spun on my heel and walked off along the sidewalk; head high and back straight; High Noon.

Well, perhaps being in a western wasn't totally out of place: I knew a couple of bad men who needed seeing to, all right. But I'd definitely have to start working on being myself before Wednesday.

Chapter Five

Wednesday night at the Empress said the lot about living in an old part of London like Thames Reach: an ancient building filled with modern kids, loads of computerized equipment cramming the creaking stage, all dust and black speakers in the boxes, and old plaster cherubs flaking down on the beat of the music. Nothing designed, just attempts at making the best of it. And outside a crowd of kids was pushing and swearing on the pavement, making the older people walk round them and pretend not to hear all the words. Different ages thrown in together, and trying not to touch.

But perhaps it's like that everywhere. I kept my eyes skinned for the Datsun, wanted to get to it a few yards down the road before it came too close, all ready to meet her with some well-spoken word her father could hear. Whatever I thought about the social problems of Thames Reach, I definitely didn't want him to think I was one of these yobs. But when the car arrived he came in fast and dropped her right outside the door into a ruck – and I had to fight my way to get to it.

I gave him a quick once-over while I opened the door. Young-looking, blue *Fred Perry*, hair blond or grey – could have been either in that light – gold identity bracelet on his wrist. Altogether, a bit smug-looking the way fathers of daughters sometimes are, as if they own something the world wants to get its hands on. I smiled, and tried to look intelligent. But he didn't really look at me. He gave her a kiss, said something I couldn't catch, and drove off. My stomach rolled over. Wendy looked really great in a short furry jacket and white trousers, but it wasn't that. And it wasn't her smile, which could defrost our freezer. It was the family kiss that somehow seemed to cut everyone out, then him driving off without even looking at me, as if these jaunts were so everyday it wasn't worth his while speaking to every different boy.

'So this is it, eh? The famous Empress. Is this where you bring all your girls?'

'Only one at a time.'

She looked at the sprawl on the pavement. 'Do they dance inside as well?'

'I think so. Do you want to find out? Or . . . ' I waved a hand to take in all the other delights of Thames Reach on a cold night.

'Yes, please.'

I held her arm and guided her through the kicking and chasing to the small entrance hall. I already had the tickets so we went straight in.

It was a real disappointment inside. I don't know what I'd expected at a disco here, but they seemed to have done just about enough to change it from what it was and not enough to make it anything special. The front half of the stalls had been swivelled round to make a couple of rows down either side, but they hadn't got rid of the audience slope, and everything seemed to be tipping down towards the front: and in the middle, which was empty except for a few kids swinging their legs over seat arms to the music, there was a midget dance floor, flashing in the disco lights, but on the tilt as well. It was just about there, too, where we'd sat and listened to the Big Fellow. All much the same, but without the soul, and all very different. At least, that ghost was done for. Besides, I was here for the here and now, not to sit and think about the past.

Bit by bit, the place filled up; the evening got going and we danced and started to talk. It's strange how much conversation you can find when you know next to nothing about someone. There's so much to find out, for a start: like what she drinks, what music she likes, how she sees everyday things. You find yourself talking about different sorts of cornflakes with all the guff of people on a chat show. In the first half hour I found out Wendy liked the Beatles, cigar smoke, blue glass and Snoopy; Frank Sinatra, the smell of new paint, and medium cooked steaks. She disliked – nothing as deep as hate – most politicians, marrow for dinner, fat stomachs, the manager at Smith's, and cold sea. I couldn't say what I gave away about myself; but I do know I gave myself permission to be pretty strong on liking different food, a bit careful on the music front, and obeyed strict orders to be dead silent on politics with a capital P. Not that I was actually falling over to sell myself short: it's just, you can't put together too serious an argument when you're having to shout as if you're in a lifeboat at sea.

It was a good time, and we both went out of our ways to find things we agreed on. Which I could have taken a lot of. Going out with someone was turning out to be a lot less nervy than I thought. And I hadn't felt the need to do my John Wayne once – till Alfie Cox sauntered in.

He came with a loud crowd of hard cases, the sort who stand in doorways and make you ask to go through: and that wouldn't have been too bad, I could have left getting another drink till they moved; but he saw me looking, and there was no way I could go on with a pantomime of pretending I didn't know he was there. He had a word with one of his gang and looked back again with his long seeing-me-out stare. I took no notice; but I couldn't stop wondering how long it'd be before he made a move. I sneaked a secret look at my watch to see if I'd seem completely mad suggesting a Wimpy and a quiet walk home: but we'd only just got there, really, and Wendy looked like she was enjoying the dances we did. And so was I. She had this way of turning into someone else when she got on the floor; she said things with her movements and her eyes that completely contradicted her Mummy and Daddy talk, and somehow I quite liked the new feeling of not being too sure where I stood. But there in the background was Alfie Cox, and trouble was written all over his pretty face.

He saved it till I went to get our second drink. Wendy was on Coke, and I'd had a cider, but dancing and talking like that are thirsty work, and after she'd done the old trick of going to drink from an empty glass the second time, I couldn't ignore it: there was no way out of making the move past that crowd at the door. 'Don't go away!' I said. I meant it as a joke; but I hadn't reckoned on her playing one back. When I came in from the bar she wasn't there: not in her seat, anyway: there she was out on the floor with Alfie Cox, and I could suddenly see why he'd given me no bother getting through.

I tried to take it in good part: I tried to tell myself he was just another bloke, anyone who might have fancied his chances while I was out at the bar. It happened all the time, I reckoned, and no harm done. If the girl was out with you she'd be polite to him, then come back after – that was the way it worked, wasn't it? But I couldn't win the argument. That was Alfie Cox out there, and he was holding her really close – closer than I'd danced tonight – and he was whispering in her ear all the rotten time.

So what sort of poison was the villain spreading? He wasn't making her laugh, that was for sure; she just nodded now and then, and once or twice she gave him one of those special dancing looks I'd thought were just for me. It was hard as hell to sit and take that: especially as he kept looking over and giving me a knowing wink: and the dance went on and on. If I hadn't cared so much I might just have got up and cleared off, walked out of there, let her have him. But I did care; so I sat and sipped at my drink and tried to kid everyone my only interest in the world was the crinkles in my glass.

'Cheer up, Saturday! I've brought your bird back.' He swung her towards me like someone off 'Come Dancing'. 'I been tellin' 'er about your skill as a market spieler. She's dyin' to 'ear you 'ave a go, i'n that right, doll?'

'Not really,' she said. But something in her face told me that may not have been what she'd said to him a minute ago.

He walked away, hitching his jeans, and his ears moved as he pulled a face for his mates. They rolled their eyes and dribbled something dirty into their beer.

'D'you know him?' I asked Wendy.

'No.'

'Looked as if you did.'

'Really? How?' She'd gone stiff, started sipping her Coke as if a waiter was hovering to know what it was like.

'You seemed to get on all right.'

'I get on all right with a lot of people. I got on all right with you at the Albion Club.'

She was putting me in my place. I hadn't known her five minutes and I was coming on strong as if I owned her.

Still, she had come out with me. 'Well, I've got my reasons, but I've got just about as much time for that bloke as I've got for leprosy.' I definitely wasn't going to take a middle-of-the-road conversational line over Alfie Cox to please her or anyone.

'He only had a laugh about your show-up. It sounded funny. I wish Sandra hadn't pulled me off to the Wimpy.'

'You weren't laughing.'

'Well, I didn't want to hurt your feelings, did I? Anyway, what were you doing watching so close?'

Another put-down. I knocked back the rest of my cider without any of it touching the sides.

'Come on, don't sulk! Forget it Kevin. Anyway –' she put her hand on top of mine – 'I bet I'd have been proud of you. At least it sounds as if you had a go. I bet you weren't *half* as bad as he said.'

I stared at the suds in my glass. 'I wasn't, as it happens, till I lost my bottle.'

'Well, have another go Saturday. I'll come and hear you specially. In my dinner break. Wait till I come and I'll get up the front of the crowd and give you an honest opinion.'

I found a smile from somewhere. 'Thanks, but don't bother. I don't reckon I'll try that again. Come on, let's dance.'

What was playing wasn't a specially slow song – the DJ definitely liked to keep people hopping – but we did it close all the same: close for us, and close for Alfie Cox. For him I went to town. I snuggled my cheek into her hair, I held her tight and shuffled us round at our own speed while the rest of the place became a blur. I smelt her perfume, felt her warmth, and really enjoyed that special feeling of dancing with her. And it was a few seconds after the music stopped before we realized we were on our own, standing there, still not wanting to pull apart.

'I think we'd better go now. They don't like me getting in too late.'

'OK.' I wanted to say something else, but I couldn't search the words out.

'Come on then, Romeo, on your bike!' She smiled, and became the other Wendy again. 'When you've gotta go, you've gotta go!' I led her off the floor and chose a moment to dive out when Alfie Cox was up at the bar. I only hoped he'd seen the dance, that was all.

I took Wendy home on the bus, holding hands all the way: out to a little road on the other side of the Wellcome roundabout where the steel grey Datsun blocked one of the drives. It was one of those thirties houses, semi-detached, big bay windows and diamond panes. Very nice, but I was much more interested in a kiss goodnight. Just as we got to the front door, though, the blessed porch light went on, and with nothing more than a brush of my face and 'See you!' she started to go in.

'When?'

'Saturday. I said I'd come round in my dinner break. 'Bout twelve.'

'OK. See you. But don't expect a performance . . . ' And she'd gone inside, back to her Daddy, and Frank Sinatra, and her blue glass.

It was a long way home, walking – but I needed the time. There was so much to go over now: a real Spaghetti Junction of feelings to try to straighten out. And up to the Wellcome roundabout the most important one was all to do with Wendy and me: running over how it had gone, the things said, the depressing depths of seeing her with Alfie and the heights of sharing that dance. But as I got nearer home and the roads became more familiar, it was Max who came more and more into my mind. Conscience, was it? Right that minute she'd be in her workroom making something out of a bit of leather. Or was it fear? Fear of what I'd promised myself I'd do for Max, and hadn't yet, something tonight's brush with Alfie Cox could easily have made ten times more dangerous.

Having Alfie as an enemy over the market stall was bad enough: but being up against him over a girl as well was going to make life diabolical. So the next Saturday was something really special to dread, a sort of black letter day.

When it came, the weather had turned from a hard freezing wind to being blustery with spatters of rain thrown at you from different directions, one of those days when you don't know whether to waterproof the stall all over and look prepared for the Thames to flood, or put the top sheet on and get quietly soaked. Either way, with the wind whipping up all over the place and people not knowing where the next wet gust was coming from, it was a morning of flapping tarpaulins and short tempers all up and down the market.

'Do you *mind*?'

'You must be bloody joking!'

'Oh, leave it out!'

You heard a lot more of that than the warm-hearted Cockney mateyness they put in American films. So, with my hair blown up from the back like a clown's wig, my hands slipping in the wet on the stall handles, and the sting of the rain in my eyes, I pulled myself along the aggravation of the High Pavement to be met by a stack of boxed saucepans stuck bang in the middle of our pitch: all carefully positioned, with a plastic sheet over them, and tons of room all round. Even if they'd been ours I wouldn't have left them just there. Naturally, the Coxes were about already, and Charlie was thumping around in the back of his van as if he was wrestling an ox in there. But Alfie was handy, leaning up on the van's side with the innocent look of someone in a Laurel and Hardy film waiting to see what would happen next.

I looked at the piled boxes, I looked at Alfie, and I banged down the stall and stood there, blocking the pavement. Both of us knew he'd have to shift his saucepans soon, once he'd got me wet, or the others trying to get by would have a go. But he took his time over doing it; the only person I've met who could put a smirk into his walk.

He was a horrible sight: soft hair, hard chin, white teeth in his open mouth and film actor eyes. Everything to make a bloke like me loathe him. And I couldn't help thinking that those big paws had pressed Wendy close.

His eyes opened up at me and I waited for the innocent explanation for his boxes being there. I'd give him that: he always provided an excuse.

'Get your end away the other night, did you, Saturday?'

I stared at him. Filth, that's what he was. He could dirty anything with his over-sexed touch. Warm, soft Wendy held close was a world away from the sort of crafty score he was on about. I wanted to back up my stall and run it into him, crutch high.

'She's not like that,' I said. But my voice was all weak with the surprise of his alley attack.

'Who says she ain't, son? She'd do me a good turn, I reckon.'

'Then you reckon wrong, you dirty bastard!'

I looked round for something to throw: saw nothing, and spat into the rain on the pavement.

'Does your mummy know what you get up to?'

'Get stuffed, Cox!'

'Be my pleasure, Saturday. Just give us 'er address!' He stood grinning at me, took out his comb to his hair, knowing I hadn't got the guts to make a move, till he heard his father thumping towards the open end of the van. Then he started to shift his saucepans, slowly. The wind spat rain back in my face and I let off a vile string of abuse and took a tight grip on the stall. I'd do for Alfie Cox one day, I swore. One day when I had the strength I'd shut up that filthy mouth somehow!

It was a miserable morning all round. Max was depressed and silent, just watching the Coxes' every move, and the trade we did wasn't enough to keep my mind off my hatred. The time dragged as painfully as that heavy stall on iced cobbles, and it wasn't till the market clock started creeping round from eleven to twelve that I could get my mind going on thoughts of seeing Wendy.

I'd looked foward to seeing her so much it had squeezed my inside dry. I'd gone to sleep three nights thinking about her, even tried to get dreams going with us both in them – woken myself up when I wasn't satisfied and tried to switch her on again. If that's what being obsessed is, then that's the way I was about Wendy. I desperately wanted to see her again, to see her smile, and to find out a bit more about where we stood. So whether or not she kept her word and came round was very important to me. After the Empress business she might have gone home and thought I was the biggest berk going.

But there were problems. Always there were problems. Alfie Cox was right next door – and then there was Max; sad Max, drinking too much all of a sudden, who could react to a girl friend just about any way in the world right now. So it was all touch and go, all in the air. Even looking forward had the edge taken off of it these days.

It was ten past twelve by the market clock when I saw her. She'd put her hair up: and God, she looked nice! A bit older – perhaps a bit too old for me – and was I glad I'd ignored Max and worn my best donkey.

And there was definitely no passing by in the crowd this time. She was on her toes looking for me, no friends in tow, and as soon as I'd fingered my hair into place I waved to her.

'Wendy! Hi!' Oh, God, I was back in the western again!

"'Lo, Kevin.' She came over, pushed her way through, a big smile that made me want to whip the old mouth organ out and play a fanfare.

'All right?'

'Yeah. Busy. They all come in our place when the weather's like this.' She was talking to me, but her eyes were on Max. 'Some kid walked off with two dictionaries just now. Great big ones.'

'Well, he won't be lost for words when he gets nicked!'

Wendy laughed, and I knew Max was watching her, too. If I had a bit of sense I'd introduce them.

'We're a bit quiet out here. As it happens, I was wondering –' But that's as far as I got. The idea of nipping off for a Wimpy didn't get aired. I'd reckoned without the sort of stroke Alfie could pull, which was dead stupid of me after what he'd said that morning: and he'd seen her all right – who hadn't, standing out in that drab crowd like a model? Now he was on his feet at the front of the stall where his old man usually stood, all smart modern gear, looking like he'd trained a spotlight on his face, and doing the business.

'Don' go away, sweetheart, not till you've seen what I've got!'

It could have been Wendy he was calling, or one of those imaginary girls they pretend to talk to in every crowd. That didn't matter, though, because she'd turned to look at him, and for a minute my chance to pull her away had gone.

'Look who it isn't!' she said.

'Now, 'ere's a lovely thing! 'Ere *is* a lovely thing!' he was going on: and with a quick twist of his wrist a small glass vase was in his hand, a beautiful looking thing about fifteen centimetres high, shaped like a genie's bottle with a narrow neck, almost clear but smoked in a faint blue swirl. 'Ain't that a treat?'

Wendy's face said that it was. And I thought so, too. But that wasn't the point. Getting her away was what I wanted to do.

'You hungry?' I asked. But she wasn't listening to me. Alfie

Cox was flicking at the rim of the vase with a hard finger nail and we all heard it ringing deep and true.

''S'right, lady, it's your genuine Scotch design.' He held it higher. 'Lovely for the mantelpiece, on your telly with a flower in it, eh? Or give one to the missus, lads – make up for being the buggers you are! Eh?'

There was a laugh – which twisted into a loud screech as Alfie suddenly dropped his precious vase.

'Whoops!'

The big smile on my face lasted half a second while it fell – and wiped itself off quick when the vase hit his work top with a crack, and instead of smashing, bounced back.

Alfie caught it expertly in his other hand.

'Eh? See? Not glass, girls, but new Duraplas, your modern replacement. Looks like glass, sounds like glass, feels like glass. But is it glass? Not on your Nelly! No more tears over broken vases, lads. No more pickin' up the broken bits an' doin' a jigsaw to stick 'em together! Everlastin', this!' He held it up and knocked it hard with the handle of a pen-knife. 'See? Unbreakable! Now, who's the first one for a bargain? 'Cos it's not a silly price I'm asking. You can keep your ten pound, keep your five pound, even your three and your two. I'll tell you what I'll do – Christ this is Mickey Mouse money I'm askin' – give me *one pound!*' He banged his top with the flat of his hand and stared at everyone, triumphant. '*One pound!* For something that'll last for ever!'

All the hands were shooting up. Suddenly Charlie Cox couldn't keep up with the rush in the crowd, throwing out the cardboard boxes, grabbing the money and shouting, 'One over there, one over there, one over there . . . '

It was impulse buying, whipped up now, as carefully staged as an opera; a really good piece of selling. Alfie Cox doing what I couldn't, and all in front of Wendy.

And all because of Wendy, no doubt about that!

I looked round at her, ready to lead her away now he'd finished impressing her. But her face was all lit up. 'Hold on a minute,' she said, and before I knew where I was she was buying one of the vases, reaching over and being handed a box with a big wink by Alfie himself.

I felt like an ant underfoot. Small and *insignificant*. Didn't she know anything about being loyal? Hadn't she got it straight by now that she was getting at me when she went along with Alfie Cox?

'Oh, it's nice.' She'd taken hers out of its box and was holding it up for me to see. She caught Max's eye with it, too. 'Isn't that lovely?'

Max stared at the plastic vase. 'If you like that sort of thing,' she said.

Alfie saw me, knowing what he'd done, and he grinned. 'Givin' 'er a treat, Saturday?' he shouted.

A customer of our own started hovering over a belt. I grabbed a handful of others and started giving him some sales talk as if my life depended on it. But it wasn't done for him. It was for Wendy, and not to impress her. More to be busy and leave her hovering.

How could she buy one? It might have been my fault, not taking the talk a bit deeper on Wednesday, not explaining about us and the Coxes; but didn't she know by now what would upset me?

There definitely wasn't any future in her and me any more.

'I'll have to get on, Kevin,' she said. 'Got to get a bite. We finish late, worse luck.'

'Yeah, OK.' I hardly looked up from the fascination of selling a belt.

'So . . . I'll see you, then?'

'Yeah, expect so.' I measured the man's waist, gave him royal treatment, and when I looked up again, she'd gone, thank God.

The man bought his belt and I dumped down on to a box. I kicked the pavement, ground my heel round in a wet scrape. I put my head in my hands. If there'd been a bottle of Bacardi there I'd have downed it, never mind Max; because I reckoned I knew how she felt now. She'd had something and it had all gone wrong; and now the same had happened to me. Wouldn't it have been better never to have known . . . ?

I heard Alfie going on. I listened to his professional cockney whine and hated him more than ever. He'd got what I hadn't, and he'd ruined what I'd had.

He was rabbiting away, but the vases had got a big crowd

together which shut us off with their backs. So I did my best to stop listening to his cocky voice, sat there kicking at the cardboard under my feet, and grubbed around in my own miserable mind. And then I heard the words. Floating over everyone's head. 'Ladies' watch' and 'Geneva': two electric shocks which shot me on to my feet. Had I heard that right? Wasn't the Geneva ladies' watch what I'd bought the other night, my shady deal at the Club for Max's birthday? I was dead certain that's what the fat man had called it. I stared across, and, sure enough, that's what it was, the same watch being held up in its long, snappy box, exactly the same stolen goods I'd bought for a quid.

'Now where else, lads, are you gonna get one of these? Accurate quartz movement, beautiful analogue face – it's got two 'ands, girl, like your ol' man – matchin' bracelet! Elegant, an' nothin' to go wrong! Fellows – picture 'er face when the lady in your life puts this on! Or the wife!' He lifted it out of its box and dangled it there in the drizzle. 'West End jeweller's bankrupt stock, fully guaranteed.' Alfie's long fingers lifted out the card to unfold it. 'An' you're all thinkin' about fifty pounds, ain't you? Well, I'll tell you, girls, you can even afford to treat yourselves today!' He put everything down except the watch, which he held up above their heads, smacking his work top with his free hand. 'Well, you can forget fifty pounds. Forget thirty, forget twenty. It's a bargain at fifteen, but I ain't even askin' ten. Tell you what I'll do – first half-dozen with their 'ands up – Gawd, this is *silly!* Give me a pound! Who wants a ladies' dress watch for a *pound*?'

They went berserk. They almost started fights to get their money out: the first half-dozen, and the next, and the next. Alfie must have sold thirty of them, Charlie grabbing the cash while the crowd was told to check their watches' accuracy by the market clock.

At first I felt sick: sick that Max would think her present was the cheap touch Alfie was shifting – which, of course, it was. But suddenly the sickness was gone and in its place was a new sort of rolling elation.

I'd got him. I'd got *them*. I'd done for the Coxes, got enough on them now to make their application for our pitch look stupid.

Stolen goods! The Coxes were dealing in stolen goods! And whatever everyone thought, the council came down on bent traders like a ton of bricks if something was proved. That watch was the same as mine: same model, same crooked price, fallen off the back of the same lorry!

And there were enough of them left in the carton at Alfie's feet to prove it when the law came round.

I didn't stop to think. I didn't wait to be put off, to risk Max's depressing hand on my shoulder. I went into action alone. 'Got to go somewhere,' I told her, and I ran off between the stalls in the direction of the public lavatories on my urgent business.

The lavatories were railed-in on an island in the middle of the road, two separate flights of steps down into the stench under the market. But in between them, up on top, was the public telephone box. That's where I was going. Never mind Simple Crooked Saunders. I was going straight to the law.

I'd never dialled 999 before – and let's face it, even at the time it did seem a bit extreme; but there were no directories in there for phoning the local station direct.

'Emergency. Which service, please?'

'Er, police. But it's not really an emergency.'

'What is the nature of your call?'

'I want to report – I know where there's some stolen goods.'

The line seemed to go dead for a moment.

'Please ring 230 1212,' the calm voice said, and clicked off in a rush to deal with more life-and-death things.

I could have stopped it then. I could easily have pushed my way out of the box and let it all drop. I was really tempted to: not getting through first time *had* to be telling me something. It should have been all over for me by now, a simple piece of information given, handed over to the police, with me back on the stall and hardly missed by anyone. But I only had to think of Alfie and Wendy and I got angry again – so it was as much for that as for helping Max that I had one more try.

The number I'd been given needed coins putting in, but it still turned out to be Scotland Yard. And within seconds I was switched to a local number, and I was informing . . .

'Station Officer here.'

'Oh. Er, I want to report some stolen goods.'

'I see, sir. Stolen from you, were they?'

'No. They're being sold. I've just seen them being sold, in the market.'

'And your name, sir?'

I made one up. It came easy, almost without thinking. 'Fellow. Jimmy Fellow.'

'And your address, sir?'

'Address? Oh, Twenty-four, London Road, Thames Reach.' It could have scared me, how easily the lies came.

'And what are these stolen goods, sir?'

I told him, and in the same breath I told him who was selling them, too.

'So just how do you know these goods are stolen, sir? You say they weren't stolen from you?'

'No. That's right. I've . . . er . . . seen them mentioned somewhere. *Police Five*, it might be, or on *Capital* . . . '

'Mmmm. Doesn't ring a bell. This wouldn't be . . . some sort of a joke, would it, Mr Fellow?'

'No!' I looked outside the box. The police station was only round the corner. In all this time they could have traced the call and sent someone round to catch me. 'I'm definitely not wasting your time. You get round the market and see. Coxes' stall. *Geneva* watches. You're always on about wanting the public to help. Well, I'm helping you . . . '

'And we're much obliged, sir. Except London Road runs out before it gets into the postal area of Thames Reach. Are you sure we have the correct . . . ?'

I slammed the phone down. I was shaking. I'd thought I'd been so clever and glib, and I hadn't: I'd tripped up over the address, and now I was suddenly wondering what else I'd done to give myself away. Had I left some tell-tale voice trace on a tape recorder? Given myself away by the name I'd chosen? I pulled out of the box, and like a blast of cold air hitting me, it suddenly struck me what I'd really done. I'd climbed over the barrier, out of the private world racing round inside my head and thrown myself full tilt into the real world of revenge and the law. And what's more, when they came – if they came – to investigate the Coxes, I'd be right next door, having to see it all happening and trying not to go red when they stared . . .

And it only needed the police to tell Cox when the call had been made, and they'd have me. The way Alfie watched, he'd know I'd been away about then.

What a stupid bloody fool! This was *real* warfare, taking on the Coxes like this. This was knife-in-an-alley stuff, hitting at the way they made a living. And I'd started something I didn't have the power to stop. All because of how I felt about Wendy buying something off Alfie.

My inside rolled right over, and it ached. I wanted to run down into that gents and be sick as a dog. But there wasn't time for a luxury like that. My only hope now was to get back to the stall and make it look as if I'd never left it.

I ran across the market, zig-zagged in and out of the stupid, hindering crowds. The idiot old women! The daft men with big bags who didn't know what they wanted! *Get out of it!* I wanted to shout. *This is my bloody life you're threatening!*

I tripped over a stupid box of bananas, skidded on some cabbage ends, and slithered back under the low tarpaulin at the back of our stall to start frantically tidying cardboard on the pavement as if I'd been down there all the time. Never been away.

The Coxes were taking their break. The crowd had gone and they were smoking into their mugs of tea.

Max had that strange look people have when they're sitting on a chair in the rain.

'Where the dickens have you been?'

'Nowhere! Down here, haven't I?' *Shut up, Max,* I wanted to say. *Shut up for crissake!*

'Nowhere?'

Alfie Cox looked round at us. He hadn't sneered his victory at me yet. But he'd probably been looking for me, to do it.

'Nearly done,' I said loudly, making no sense. 'God, it don't half make your back ache under here.'

I heard Alfie laugh, and cough up tea, and start to do 'Love Story' in loud dooby-do's. He knew I'd been off somewhere, all right. All he'd got wrong was the reason – for the time being.

It was surprising how quickly the police came; it scared me stiff; quarter of an hour at the most. There were two of them, one white and one black, young men, CID written all over their anoraks. And they didn't hang about. With no selling going on, they went straight up to the old man.

"'Ello, Col.' Charlie Cox slapped the tall white one like family. 'Charlie.'

'What can I do for you? Something for that lovely lady o' your'n.' You could just see old Charlie – guest of honour at the Policeman's Ball.

Alfie stood back on one side, flipping a lighter and watching the black man's eyes.

'Got any watches, Charlie? Ladies'?'

'Yeah, got some somewhere. Knocked some out just now.' Charlie's hand dipped into the carton and pulled out a long box. "'Ave a look at one o' these, Col.' Charlie took the watch out of its box and gave it to the CID man, who looked at it and checked it against something written on a piece of paper.

'How much you knocking these out for?'

'A quid to punters. Nice little number, that. I can do you one for eighty-five an' break me heart.'

'Yeah? That's cheap.'

'It is. But that's all I've got. I ain't got nothing dearer today. Reckon it'll do?'

'Oh, it's not to buy, Charlie, sorry. Have you got a chitty for these?'

Even from where I was, under our stall, I could see Charlie look at him with one of those expressions that say you suddenly understand everything. 'As if I wouldn't!' he said, and shuffled into the van, while the other three stood still, with Alfie trying like hell to look innocent. Next door, I was doing my best just to keep breathing. Because this was it, this was the crunch. This was when Charlie was going to have to come out and say he couldn't find the receipt, when the first step got taken to put these two in the shade. I shivered down my back. It was electric, like waiting for the Big Fellow to come out and take a solo. Except I'd written the music to this one . . .

"'Ere y'are.' Charlie came back and rifled through a bull-dog clip of invoices. 'Smith an' Stacey, Romford Broadway.'

Both detectives looked at it carefully. Charlie waited. So did I. It couldn't be a moment before the paper was queried.

'Something up, Col?'

'No, Charlie, don't look like it. How do they do it at this price?'

'What, a quid? Taiwan, ain't it? They're floodin' the market, these. Cheap labour, strong pound, an' watches ain't what they was in value years gone by, not without the good in the cases. Bit o' tin, bit o' quartz, bit o' plastic. Don't really amount to much.'

'Is that it?' The black detective looked hard at the watch on his own wrist. 'I was wonderin' why me arm was goin' green.'

Alfie grinned. 'Thought you was changin' colour, did you?'

'Had me worried, son!'

The others laughed, but Charlie Cox was frowning. 'Someone fingerin' me, Col?' he asked, in the sort of quiet voice people use when they're holding a gun.

'No, I don't reckon. Someone wondering why they was so cheap, that's all. Sold many today?'

'Fair few.'

'Not bad, then. No wonder you run a Roller.'

'Someone made a complaint?'

There was a second's silence while I wanted the High Pavement to open up and quietly drop me down a sewer out of sight. Me and my brilliant scheme for getting the Coxes in bother!

'No – just some happy punter with a bargain, I reckon. Trying to put a stop to too many sharing his good luck.'

Charlie shrugged, and Alfie started shifting some cartons. It was no real hassle to them, I told myself, not this sort of thing when they were in the clear. It probably happened all the time.

'Well, thanks a lot, Charlie.' But Col didn't go straightaway. He'd just seen something else. 'Here, these real leather?' Insult to injury – he'd picked up one of the briefcases Cox had taunted me with the week before.

Charlie took it back, squeezing the plastic wrapping in his big hand. 'Well, they are, but – you know . . . ' He took a quick look across in our direction. 'Won't last; not man enough for you . . .'

'No?'

Charlie threw it out of sight inside his van, and as quickly as they'd come the two CID disappeared. And suddenly I started taking this enormous interest in tidying our stall. Head down, hands busy, I did anything to stop me having to look their way – like a kid who gets madly on with his work when he's been spotted up to something through the classroom door.

I was scared, and I was sick, too. Sick at my failure. Having taken that huge chance it should have been enough to have done for the Coxes. Instead of which they'd seen off the police like a couple of old mates.

In a very low key I started whistling to myself. Something I'd been making up in my bedroom for mouth organ and a slow, tapping foot. 'High Pavement Blues', I called it. Just a tune; no words; but with a hell of a lot of meaning.

Chapter Six

If it's all right to steal food when you're starving, then it's all right to go looking for comfort when you're miserable. There comes a time for everyone when they can swallow their pride and go off after what they want. Which was my excuse for going round to Smith's after we'd packed up.

And I had been a bit hard on Wendy, hadn't I? Perhaps she was so sure of herself she didn't know what it was like to feel jealous. If she never had feelings like that herself, how could I expect her to know the way I felt when she had dealings with Alfie Cox? Well, whatever the truth of it, she was just about all I had going for me, and I felt low enough after that watches business to give her more than the benefit of the doubt.

I ran round into Hudson Street and just squeezed into the shop before closing, practically under the manager's arm as he started bolting off the doors.

'Hey – we're just on closing.'

"S'all right, won't be a tick. I know what I want.'

I took the stairs two at a time, nearly butted Old Lavender in the stomach as she came down gripping her handbag tight.

'Look where you're going!'

'Sorry.' I raced on up. At least *she'd* be out of my way this time.

Wendy had her coat on ready, tidying a shelf of maps, with her back to me. I took a deep breath and walked casually over to her. John Wayne again.

'Need any help making your mind up where to go?' I asked her.

'You mean right this minute or when I've got my Porsche?' She didn't even look round.

'I mean – like – tonight.'

'Oh.' She blew the dust off a road atlas of France. 'You thinking about fish and chips in Monte Carlo?'

'No, I'm thinking about a disco at the Albion Club.'

She still wouldn't look round. She was bantering with me,

but she was definitely holding off. I tossed up between carrying on and going home. I could do without a moody from her: that wasn't what I'd come for. It was a very close thing, because as I shrugged my shoulders to go, she turned round, put her weight on one foot and stared at me.

'Go with a crowd, you mean?'

'I was thinking just you and me.'

'Oh, I dunno about that. I'd made up my mind to go out with Sandra and the others.'

'It's up to you, o' course. But it's a bit off, one bloke and a crowd of girls. Besides, I want to say something to you.'

She looked back at the maps. 'I don't want to get too serious, Kevin.'

'That's all right.' I wasn't ready to get married, either. 'I was going to tell you about Alfie Cox and me, that's all.'

'Why? You haven't got to.'

'I know, but I want to.'

'Oh.' She flicked a map book out and in, out and in on its shelf.

'Well, what d'you reckon?'

'All right, then. What time?'

'Half-past seven?'

She looked at a bare wrist. 'What's the time now?'

'Just on six.'

'All right. Half-past seven, then, outside the Albion Club.'

A bell rang throughout the store, low and slow, so people didn't start diving for the fire exits.

'That's it: we've got to go. I'll see you tonight. But I don't want any more wobbles,' she said. She looked at me straight, and skidded out under my arm for the stairs.

I followed her. The same man was holding the last door open, everyone going out under his arm like oranges and lemons.

'Goodnight, Wendy,' he said, with a hot little look.

'Goodnight, Mr White. Have a nice weekend.' She gave *him* her smile, too: Mr White, the same manager she'd told me she disliked so much.

So that was it! I didn't understand her, but I was getting nearer. Just a front, this top smile was; and that's why Alfie Cox could come in for it. Him, and the rest of the world. Just politeness: which still left room for her to be special to me. Didn't it?

And that thought made me feel a bit better. All the same, I managed to knock White's arm with my shoulder, made his hand slip down the door. Level the score a bit, I thought: balance her politeness with my bad manners.

'Here – '

'Sorry, mate.' But I wasn't. After my day I wasn't prepared to be sorry for anyone except me.

And I didn't fancy leaving too much to chance either. Nick's house wasn't too far out of my way, so after seeing Wendy jump in Daddy's car, I headed for it. It was one of those modern little maisonettes on the new estate where the dockyard used to be. There wasn't room to swing a cat in it, but since they didn't allow cats that didn't seem to bother anyone. Even so, it seemed more claustrophobic than ever when Nick's little sister tried to open the door and it jammed against his outsize rucksack at the bottom of the stairs. God knows what he found to put in it.

She didn't ask me in: just yelled, 'Nick!' and left me standing there.

Nick came down the stairs as far as he could and leaned over the banister.

'Wotcha, Kev!'

It was a friendly word, and it bucked me up. We'd drifted a bit apart, Nick and I. We'd been through juniors together and gone up through the comprehensive, but he'd taken something of a back seat this last week or two since I'd had Wendy on my mind. I suppose that happens. Anyway, he'd been a good mate, Nick.

'What can I do for you, my son?'

'Not a lot, if you're leaving home!'

Nick put two fingers up at the clutter in the hall. It looked as if all the house was there to be packed up in his rucksack. 'You'd think we was going to the South Pole, the way she goes on. But it's Seaford, isn't it? Half-term, week after next – or had you forgot?'

I hadn't. It was four days away from home – Friday till Tuesday night – that I'd had glowing in front of me like the light from an air shaft in the middle of a long tunnel. Away at the sea doing beach profiles, the wind blowing in my face, a Saturday away from the market and Alfie Cox, staying in a hostel with a few of the lads. It looked like being a really good laugh. And I'd vaguely heard Nick saying he was going to get his gear out and check it tonight: I definitely wouldn't have called if I'd thought he was free.

'I'll have to sort some stuff out sometime. But I haven't got a rucksack . . . '

'Get your mum to knock you one up.'

'No, old sports bag'll do for Seaford.' The trouble with Nick was, he always had to look the part: wore the full England kit if we went for a kick-around in the park. Still, that was to my advantage tonight . . .

'Anyhow, don't tell me you've come to help sort me out . . . '

'No, I do draw the line somewhere. I came to see if your dad was going down the Albion Club tonight . . . '

'Why, you going?'

'I was thinking about it.'

'He's not in yet. He might. But you won't have no trouble getting in. Just give his name, they know you down there.'

'Yeah. Sure . . . '

'Why, something special, is it?'

I didn't really want to tell him, but there was no way out. 'I might go down with that Wendy. Just thought it'd be nice if I definitely knew your dad was going.'

Nick leaned back off the banister. He was a weird bloke when he wasn't the centre of your attention. 'Don't know what you see in her. Anyhow, I'll tell him when he gets in.'

'Cheers. And the best of British with the kitchen sink. Here, leave room for a few ciders . . . '

'Shut up!' Nick hissed. 'Or she won't let me go. I've had to tell her there's teachers going as it is.'

'See you, then.'

'Yeah, see you.'

I shut the door for him, pulled it on myself, with that rotten feeling you get when you've been trying to make sure about something and you've only made it worse. Nick wasn't going to say a word to his dad – unless it was something negative. A mistake, I decided. Just one of tons I seemed to be making these days.

When I got in Max was standing over a soup saucepan at the stove, all stiff and ready to have a go. You could always tell by the way she stood with her shoulders up. Also, she'd already had her first Bacardi, going by the glass; probably her second; and the scene was set for something.

Before all this, she'd always worked things out on her leather. She'd say so herself: talk about punching out her aggro on her thonging holes, stamping her opinions with a die, shaping some new idea with a sharp knife. Quite literary she got, sometimes, going on about it. But in the past couple of weeks she'd done a lot more sitting and staring, or sitting and drinking. And to think that if I'd done for the Coxes today, she could have been singing away at her table right now! Instead of which . . .

'That's two of the stupidest tricks you've ever pulled, Kevin, two weeks running.'

I frowned, all innocent. 'What do you mean?'

'You know what I mean. Last week you came the big salesman. Now you go running to the police.'

'Eh? Who said?'

'No one said. *I* said. I just know – and so do you. And Cox isn't stupid, either. What d'you take him for?' She shook salt into her soup with an angry jerk, almost losing hold of the packet.

I stared at her, about ready to back down: but an anger of my own was rising at the unfairness of her attack. 'Well, you tell me,' I said, all thin in my throat, 'do you want that pitch or don't you?'

'What?'

'"Cos *you're* doing sweet Fanny Adams about it!'

For a second I thought the saucepan of soup was coming all over me. If it hadn't been so hot I think it would have; I could see throwing it go through her mind as she screwed her face up.

'I want the pitch!' she screeched. 'You bloody know I want the pitch!'

'Do you?' I let go, too: all that built-up aggravation. 'Then why don't you do something about it? Instead of having a go at me. Instead of feeling sorry for yourself and drinking yourself silly?!'

The salt packet came first. Then the soup, clanging against the door as I slammed it on the kitchen and held it tight, suddenly shaking with where we'd got. I *heard* the mess. And all of Thames Reach heard the scream as she started to kick at the door. But I screamed above all the noise she could make, heart going, lungs heaving: 'At least I'm trying!'

There was silence, then a cry, a high wail, and the scrape of a chair.

I waited till I heard her whimpering, and then I went back in. I knew I'd gone too far. I deserved to risk anything else she wanted to sling at me.

'I'm sorry.' My feet sucked at the mushroom slush on the cork floor. 'I'm sorry, Max.'

'Kevin . . .' She was hunched, pathetic, and now all I wanted to do was to put my arm round her and squeeze her: a son's squeeze, for me and for her, and the first she'd had in two years.

I started to cry, too. 'I didn't mean it,' I said. 'I know you're trying to . . . do what's best . . .'

'I don't know . . .' she grizzled, and we rocked each other, her sitting, me bending over, squeezing and swaying and doing without words.

My eyes were running, so was my nose, and in all that emotion I suddenly heard myself asking something I'd never been able to ask her before.

'Why did he go, Max? What made him go?' It was the first time I'd felt ready to hear the answer.

She stopped crying for a minute. She pulled her stained fingers slowly down her face and looked at me with her tired, red eyes.

'I've been . . . asking myself that for eighteen months.' She took in a long, shaky breath. 'If it was . . . some other woman . . . some bit of a girl from the NAAFI . . . I don't think I'd have minded so much . . .'

I squeezed her again. 'It *was* just his music, then . . . ?'

'His music, and *him* . . . Oh, Christ, look at that soup!'

70

'Good job it wasn't tomato!'

'He couldn't take . . . not being someone. The band, a bit of rank, the solos. When he came out he reckoned he was just another grey old face in Thames Reach.'

I was trying to grasp it, trying to get hold of something she hadn't got hold of herself. 'But he played . . . '

'Oh, the odd Sunday, always a favour they did him . . . '

'He came out, though. He could've stayed in . . . ' What I meant was, he could have gone against her wishes.

'Oh, yes, he came out. I made him. But only because I didn't want to lose him to a bomb in Ireland. I bullied him to do it . . . '

I looked at her puffed, lidded eyes, the thickened skin; and I suddenly realized I'd seen her move on an age tonight. She'd crossed over a line, there in front of me.

'Well, perhaps he . . . feels sorry about going now . . . '

'I hope he does!' She went stiff, her voice came hard again. 'If *we* weren't enough for him. If our family life didn't boost him enough. The self-centred great kid!'

I let go my grip a bit. The backs of my legs and my shoulders were starting to ache from bending over to cuddle her.

'He still sends the money . . . '

'A cheque from the agent, not even his writing on it.'

We both knew the Richmond postmark that was on the monthly allowance envelope.

'I still don't see why we can't use him to help us. We take his money –'

'That's our right.'

'Well, what's the difference? I don't see the diff –'

'The money's legal. Anything else is asking a favour. That's the difference. And you won't catch me asking him a favour, Kevin, not if he's the last person on earth.'

Her voice was stronger now, and there was no point going on with it. Anyway, I had to stand up. A coldness came when we stopped touching, and I swore at my aching limbs because more than anything else I wanted to make sure she knew how much someone cared.

Hell! And I was supposed to be going out in half an hour! What was the minimum time it took to show your mother how much you cared?

I slid my boots off, took three stepping stones through the soup and led her into the living room: sat her on the settee and gave her a kiss, then scuttled out to clean the floor and wipe the paint down like a madman while I made a pot of tea.

What a situation! So what was I going to do about Wendy and tonight? I could phone her, but the trouble was, she'd be almost ready to come out, and it didn't matter how serious I made it sound, after today, and coming all at the last minute, it would just about finish us off. On the other hand, there was no way I ought to be going out. I really should stay in: I *had* to stay in, for God's sake – perhaps just pop out for some Chinese for the two of us, then watch the telly with Max and share the evening. My heart sank into my boots at the thought of it. Which left nothing but homework to stare at on Sunday, and no more Wendy. But I knew what I had to do. It hurt: but Kevin Kendall had to put himself second from now on.

I'd got to show I was different to the Big Fellow.

I groaned out loud. One or two moments I'd had with Wendy had been good while they lasted. But I had to make that phone call, and there was no way I could make it sound all right to stand her up. Oh, God!

I poured the tea and pushed at the door; and I stopped. The tea slopped hot on my hand, but I hardly felt it – because I'd suddenly seen there was another way! Right! There was usually another way if you had the cool to let it come. What if I just took half an hour to meet Wendy and explain things to her? That'd be better than a phone call, and I could easily do it in the time I'd take to get Chinese. It would definitely show her I'd taken the trouble. It would leave the door open, and still give me the evening at home with Max. It was a nothing solution, and my belly was still going over with disappointment, but it was better than losing out all round, wasn't it?

I gave Max what was left of her tea. 'Anything good on telly tonight?' I rubbed my hands and tried to look all bright.

'I don't know. Is there ever?'

'Well, doesn't matter. I don't mind a bit of rubbish. How about, I'll get some Chinese, and we'll sit round?'

She looked up at me, but there was no chance of her mood

letting her smile; not even a sad one. 'I couldn't eat a thing, Kevin.'

'No? OK. *San fairy*. But I'll just nip out for a few minutes, tell someone what I'm doing.'

'Were you going out, then?'

'Yeah, but nothing special. It's just, I can't get them on the phone.'

'Not Nick, then?'

'No. Someone else.'

She put her mug down and gave me a long drawn-out sigh. 'Listen, Kevin, honestly, I really just want to put my feet up for half-an-hour; then there's one or two things I want to do. You go out. It's nice of you to think of me.' She gripped my wrist and squeezed it. 'Really. I'll be all right. Honest. Listen, I'll be upset if you *don't* go out.'

I looked at her; her damp curls, market jumper, patched jeans, her puffy face. She was a rotten liar.

'Are you sure?' And that was all the fight I put up. Just one *Are you sure?* I let her words persuade me instead of her face. I pretended to myself that I was convinced.

'I'm sure, Kev. Hundred per cent. Honest.'

'Only if you are.'

'I am. What, d'you want it on the Bible?'

'Well . . .'

'Oh, on your bike, Kev! Go on.'

I heard her dry mouth go in a try at a smile: but I wasn't looking. I was edging to the door: over the moon with the let off: ashamed as hell at taking it.

'OK, then. Kitchen's cleared. See you before I go.'

I got ready without wasting a single movement, a splashy wash, a half dry, into my clothes like some fireman running to grab for the brass pole. A quick look in the mirror as I scooped along the floor of the wardrobe for my best trainers – and knocked out the long jewellers' box, spinning on to the rug.

I squeezed that hateful shape fit to crush it. I snarled at it like a frightened dog at the thought of what Alfie Cox would do to me if ever he saw Max or me with what was inside it. Then I crammed it into my donkey jacket. Max would have no use for this on her birthday now, anyway. There was only one place for this. Down the nearest drain: or in the river.

The hand in my pocket was meant to look all casual to her as I said cheerio: but at least the worry of what was under it covered up the guilt I had, going.

'I'm off, then . . .'

Her elbow was on the chair arm, her head in her hands like a teacher in Prayers.

'Eh?'

'If you're really *sure* you're all right . . .'

'Oh, yes. 'Course I am.'

'Won't be too late.'

'Yes.' She wasn't with me at all: her mind was miles away.

The same aggravating rain blew at me as I crossed Rope Street and headed for the river. I turned my collar up and did my Humphrey Bogart again. The side streets were almost empty, but there were one or two people about, and I must have looked weird as I hurried along the pavement and slowed down at every trickle of water. The watch was burning a hole in my pocket, there was no way I could relax till I'd lost it down a drain. Not that it was stolen, or even stolen goods received – far from it! All the same, getting rid of something like that could have the same suspicious look about it as losing a terrorist's gun. There was no innocent-looking way of taking a jewellers' box out of your pocket, bending down by a drain and dropping it in.

The trouble was, when there were people about I couldn't hang about at the drains for long; and when there weren't, I kept imagining these eyes staring at me out of the shadows. Stopping and bending was just too much to do. My heart got up in my mouth as I nearly did it, twice. But I failed. At the last second each time I panicked – and in the end I gave up trying and made my mind up to leave it till later when the buses had stopped running. That late, I'd be sure whether there was anybody about or not. I pulled my hankie out of my jeans pocket and packed the box flat under it. Then, with a good loud swear at Alfie Cox and the old man for everything they were doing to us, I put my head down and ran the last two streets to meet Wendy.

She was there before me. Just. As I ran up to her I saw the wide bright tail-lights of a Datsun disappear round the corner. She must have seen me coming and given Daddy the OK to go.

'Sorry if I'm late.'

'I was a bit early.'

She smiled at me, and she kissed me on the mouth; quick like your mother does, but it made me feel a whole lot better straightaway. Suddenly, I was very glad I'd come.

The dark floodlights towered up above us; under our feet we tripped on the beer cans that had wound-up the yobs that afternoon at the match. Like a proper boy friend I put my arm round her shoulder and walked her in through the big gates, over to the dingy club building behind the north terrace.

'Here, Wend, hope these cinders don't ruin your disco dancing!'

'Oh, that's good news – we are going to dance as well as talk.'

'Why not? My dad had an uncle who could do three things at once. Lived at the seaside, near the front. Reckoned he could sit on the lavatory, read the paper, and listen to the band of the Brigade of Guards all at the same time!'

Wendy laughed. 'What tune?'

'Have to be "Thunder and Lightning Polka", wouldn't it?'

She threw her head back and did a high, shocked laugh – and like that we fell in through the outside door.

Stopping dead, like some hugging statue. A table had been dragged across the middle of the entrance hall, one of those bar tables covered with a green cloth; and sitting behind it, leaning on their elbows, were two men. I knew one of them: the secretary who'd called me 'Kev' last time. The other one I'd never seen before, an older man in a suit and an overcoat, the sort you see talking union business on the news. In front of them was a large book and a neat pile of new membership cards.

'Evening. May I see your card, please?' the secretary asked me, all official, no sign that he knew me.

I even made a move toward my pocket. 'I . . . er . . . ' I turned Wendy with my arm, facing away from them. 'Have you got one?' I muttered.

'No. I thought you were a member.'

I turned back to brave it out. 'I usually come with Mr Nicholson,' I said, knowing full well that the secretary knew. 'Mr Nicholson and Nick. I . . . er . . . they said they'd be here tonight.' I looked at my watch.

Still acting official, the secretary scrutinized the signing-in book, running his finger nail down a short list of names.

Wendy breathed out loudly and stood lop-sided, the way she had in Smith's.

'No, son, I'm afraid Mr Nicholson isn't in the club at the moment. Not yet. You can wait for him that side if you want to.'

'Oh.' I looked at Wendy. 'What shall we do? Wait for Nick's dad here or come back later?'

She shrugged.

'We'll come back later,' I said, and led her out by the hand. 'Christ, I'm sorry about that.' We stood by a stack of crates where the water wasn't dripping off the gutter. 'He let me in last time. They must be having a check-up.'

'It did look a bit like it.'

With a daddy like hers, I thought, I bet she's used to getting in wherever she wants to go. But she could try to make it all right by being nice about it. 'You came before,' I attacked, 'aren't you a member, either?'

'We came with Sandra. She sorts it out.'

'Good old Sandra!' I shoved my hands in my pockets, one down deep and the other on top of what was in it, and I racked my brains for somewhere decent to go. The trouble was, for all the way they went on about the kids gathering on street corners and getting up to no good, the people who ran Thames Reach did sweet nothing for us. There was the Empress, the porno pictures or the pubs. Small wonder we got written off as a violent, drunken lot.

'Let's have a wander, then,' I suggested. 'We'll find somewhere to go.' But even as I said it I could hear my voice coming out weak with its lack of conviction.

'If you like . . . ' Her offhand mood seemed to just about match mine.

Well, Alfie Cox ruled out the Empress, I definitely didn't feel up to risking a pub, and the pictures would have been no place to talk, anyway, so we walked away from the Albion going

76

nowhere in particular, ignoring the rain – and also each other. Like with any pair on their last date, our hands didn't touch, and our thoughts must have been a million miles apart. It had all been a big mistake, this. I should never have left poor old Max tonight, and I was being paid out for it by a really awkward situation with a girl who didn't understand. How could I talk to her about the threat of Alfie if she wasn't going to be sympathetic?

As if my feet were responding to something my mouth dare not suggest, I found myself walking Wendy through the Albion back-streets, along the new orbital road and past the Catholic church, till eventually we found ourselves at the one-six-one bus stop by the Royal Artillery parade ground: a fare stage on Wendy's way home.

Accepting where we were without comment, she walked inside and leaned herself moodily against the scratched plastic window.

The rain had come on heavier. Over the road on the parade ground it was slanting across like a troop of cold, thin soldiers.

'Nice night out!' she suddenly said.

I grunted, meaning I agreed, and that went for whether she meant the pouring rain or her and me. It would have been nice to put her straight; but talking to her, explaining things, was hard to get into with the moods we were in. In any case, another thought had come to fill the front of my mind as I stood and stared out at that sheet of wet, black tarmac.

'My dad used to play up here,' I said. 'Royal Artillery Band.' I hadn't realized I'd spoken. But a sudden picture of him had come to me, standing up proud in his scarlet tunic to take a solo, sun flashing on his silver trumpet, his head held up to bounce the sound off the long building and send it back amplified. It was something I'd seen him do many a time: a trick only the drums seemed to know, using the front to get an echo, a real note and the ghost of one, two for the price of one; and hard as it was for him keeping time, it worked like a dream in the slow march tunes.

Wendy suddenly shivered: made a noise in her throat. 'Here! Look at him watching us!'

'Who? Where?'

'Over there!'

It was only an army picket, caped in the rain, patrolling the parade ground perimeter with his pick handle. But the white blob of his face was firmly fixed on the two of us across the road at the bus stop.

'Do you reckon he thinks we're IRA?'

She'd knocked my memory clean away: but at least some of her sulks seemed to have gone with it.

'I s'pose he's got to think everything. Not a job I'd fancy . . .'

A scared soldier on his own in the rain: perhaps right that minute wondering if he'd be going for a mug of cocoa at the end of his spell, or be carried into the barracks riddled with coach-bolts and six inch nails from a bomb left in a bus shelter. That sort of thing had to go through his mind simply because that sort of thing happened. A thought which put things into perspective a bit for me. If the Big Fellow had been persuaded to come out of the army by Max, he must have admitted to feeling scared at times, mustn't he? So why the devil couldn't I? I was as entitled to my fears as my father or that picket were to theirs. It wasn't unmanly to talk about fear of an enemy, was it? And hadn't I come out tonight intending to talk about mine?

But the big thing was, when Wendy had jumped at the sight of the picket she'd suddenly sounded much more like her old self.

In a strange sort of way, that seemed to be the cue: being where we were with all those memories, and Wendy unexpectedly slipping a hand into mine, as if she knew all I needed was a start. And without knowing I was going to do it, the words suddenly just seemed to come. And when they did, very natural and understandable it all sounded – not to say a bit smooth, but I think Wendy saw round that. There at the bus stop, and a bit later on the empty one-six-one I told her everything, about the Big Fellow going, about the Coxes and the licence, and about Max's sudden dive. I even got in the dismal story of the watch, and more as a token of my fear than as a gift, I gave it to her, asked her to keep it. She took it without a word, slid it into her pocket while everything came pouring out. She listened to it all, just the odd, 'Oh' and a squeeze of my hand; and by the time I'd got to the bit about a life-and-death war with Alfie she was looking as scared as I was.

We were holding very tight by the time we got to her porch, as if we'd never let each other go.

'I'll make sure no one sees the watch,' she said. 'Poor Kevin.' And then, 'Come in for a coffee, it's not late,' and before I could stop her she was opening the front door.

I stepped on to the mat as cautious as next door's cat. I wasn't at all sure Mummy and Daddy would feel as sorry for me as she did. But she led me in with all the bounce in the world.

Wendy Goodchild's house was everything ours wasn't: it was tidy, it had carpets, and it was only for living in – all soft-lit alcoves, holiday souvenirs and thin white radiators actually switched on because there was nothing stacked against them. There were no boxes of goods in the hall; no clutter; and the smell was of heather, not leather. But it was up the stairs that made you blink. Wendy had said she liked blue glass – well, now I could see where it came from. It was like a cathedral in there, the peaceful blue glow that shone through a hundred back-lit vases and ornaments. They were all the way up the stairs, with the deepest glow of all coming from a standard on the landing, made from a round old-fashioned police lamp.

It took my breath away. But I found just enough of it to say, 'No unbreakable plastic, I hope.'

'There won't be,' said Wendy.

Her parents were in the front room watching the telly, but again it was different; they were sitting up instead of lounging, actually following a programme instead of fighting sleep.

I was surprised. They were very nice people. They got up and shook hands and made room for Wendy and me on the settee. I was very impressed. Her mother was the sort you could fancy yourself, young and pretty with bright eyes, and her father was as laid-back as a golf pro whose only worry is perfecting his putt. He looked me in the eye, called me Kevin every time he spoke, and listened to the rubbish I talked as if it was actually worth hearing. I'd been all wrong about him, I decided. He was all right.

We saw the end of their play and then we sat in silence through the news. A lot of it was political, and no one wanted to start anything. But we all came to life when Thames Reach Albion got a mention again. It was the usual sort: a league game they'd played at home against Millwall and scraped through with a draw: but it wasn't so much the football as the scraping up of bodies off the terraces that made the news. No wonder they'd been having a go over membership at the club earlier on!

Wendy's dad looked at me and raised his eyebrows. 'Could 've been a bit dodgy, then, down there?'

'Yeah. It didn't seem too bright to stay . . .'

When he collected the cups and got up to go, I shifted too; but a sharp nudge from Wendy got me staying where I was on the settee.

'Nice to have met you, Kevin.'

Mrs Goodchild got up, too. 'Come again, won't you?' and with, 'Don't be too late now, Wendy,' they went out and closed the door quietly behind them.

I tried to put my finger on what I was nervy about, because all of a sudden I felt my stomach rolling over in that comfortable room: unsure of myself: jumpy. Was it being left on my own with Wendy for the first time ever? You heard about kids who made fools of themselves with a real girl. Or was I still suffering from the big fright of what I'd started with the Coxes?

Or was it something else? I remember the time Nick and I had terrible school reports to take home, one Christmas after a half term when we'd mucked about solid in all the lessons. They were just what we deserved, the come-uppances we'd thought we were too well-liked to get. To put off the dreadful moment I'd gone home with Nick to be there when his mum and dad read his, the outsider in the house to stop them getting angry. And I'd been really knocked over with how reasonable they were about it. They ticked us both off for letting ourselves down, but really they took Nick's and my side against the school. 'No sense of humour, your teachers,' his dad said. 'Should've seen what I got up to at school!' And that was it. Nick had heard the last of it. But while he relaxed and smiled, made jokes and told me not to worry, I knew damn well I was in for a lot worse than he'd got. I'd have swapped families like a shot that afternoon, mums and dads, the lot – knowing how it was all all right in that house but how it wouldn't be in mine. And by God I'd been right. Nick had come home with me, to do for me what I'd done for him, but they must have guessed we were up to something because they wouldn't even look at the report while he was there. Just put it on the mantelpiece and waited for him to go. But when he had they'd read it and given me the biggest bollocking of my life. Actual shouts from the Big Fellow and tears from Max – and that report was dragged up again and again for months. And every time it was, I thought about Nick and his family: and I got to know – for the first time, I suppose – how differently the same things hit different people; how people are never really in anything together. *Your* report is *your* report; *your* performance in a piece is *your* performance; and in the end everything's down to what *you* do, and what things do to *you*.

And I felt the same now, at Wendy's. I knew what it was, all right. Everything in the garden was rosy up here; there were no problems in the Goodchilds' house; Wendy was used to all this comfort; but my circumstances were different, and there was no way all this easy living could apply to me. The real truth of it was, I didn't feel at home.

All the same, I kissed her. I just turned my head and kissed her. Not very passionate, it was more of a peck on the side of her mouth to see how she'd react. And I was still so churned up inside I didn't know whether to be pleased or sorry when she made a little noise in her throat, slid over sideways, and pulled me down with a hand round the back of my neck. I could feel the blood beginning to rush in my ears, and getting a breath was suddenly something I had to think about and time right, like in swimming. Another problem: if you're sitting next to somebody with your faces level, and the other one leans over sideways, you have to get up and move or you end up with your face a foot away from hers. And that can be embarrassing.

I shifted, crawled into a new position, sort of lying half on top of her, and tried to concentrate on the second kiss – while my mind was half on the door opening behind me.

But I soon forgot that. I didn't know you could kiss for so long. I didn't know you could still breathe while you pressed, let go, said something quiet, and pressed again; that your lips, tongue and teeth could all get involved in this long, warm, *meeting* that went on for ever. On and on. I'll never forget that kiss; its taste, and what it stood for, and its real comfort.

Kids at school always boast about how far they get with girls, they go on about the things they're supposed to have done, the points they've scored. But I felt a million miles away from all that, that first time on the settee. That wasn't in the same world as Wendy and me. Believe it or not, nothing like that came into it, wasn't in our thoughts. We didn't want any more than that long kiss. It seemed to roll us into one, and I couldn't see how anyone who'd shared something like that could ever become a stranger to the other person. Like, walk past them in the street. There was a taste to it which I'd have to the end of my life.

So much for neither of us wanting to be serious!

At last, the sound of a cat being called in by Mrs Goodchild sat us up: but we'd been going to sit up already. It was as if we'd shown what we wanted to show each other, and that was enough. There was no doing up of clothes, no embarrassed looks or guilty giggles; we just sat there and stared into each other's eyes.

Wendy put a finger on my lips. 'Your mum's got it wrong,' she whispered. 'I don't want you beaten up or frightened by those Coxes . . . ' I kept staring; didn't know where this was leading. 'I think you need your dad back here.'

'Yeah . . . ' For at least three reasons straight off the top I knew she was right.

'Then it's up to you. You've *got* to get him back. Get him to sort it out – even if she doesn't have to know. It's not her asking a favour if she doesn't know about it, is it?' She stroked my cheek. 'Then you'll be set for years, and the Coxes can forget getting you, if your dad's around . . . '

'Yeah . . . ' Those were two of my reasons. The third she wouldn't know about, till she missed it one day. Just seeing my dad again.

'*Do* something, Kevin,' she said. 'Look after yourself.'

I looked at her and pecked her on the cheek. Even in that dim light I could see how red her mouth was, and mine felt all swollen up with the pressure of that kiss. I wanted to kiss her again, but if I did there'd be no talking for a week.

I got up and found my coat and put it on without our fingers losing touch. I said goodnight in a hoarse sort of voice, and tiptoed out of there on a pair of feet that hardly seemed to touch the ground.

Chapter Seven

As Wendy's front door closed behind me a pelt of cold rain hit hard and cleared my head like sudden, bad news. I'd actually lost those terrible churnings for half an hour, they'd disappeared without me feeling them go like a pain will after tablets, but suddenly they were back to poke me in the stomach and remind me that while I'd been deep down in that settee, other things were a long way from being all right. Alfie and Charlie Cox were still there for a start. But even worse than that, hadn't I gone off out for my own selfish reasons, grabbed with a pair of greedy hands at Max saying she was all right, when all the time I knew damn well that she wasn't? There was no denying it. And now the party was over – like in the old Bassey record. I couldn't push Max to the back of my mind as if she was a muddle in a drawer, not for a moment longer.

In a sudden panic I put my head down and ran like a vandal to get home fast. It was a hard run. The roads were miles longer than they'd seemed before; the soft cuddle had taken the running out of my legs; and drawing enough breath to keep me going was hard as a marathon in that stinging rain. Every metre seemed like two, and every slope had turned into a hill. But at last, sucking in enough breath for a hundred mouth organs, and feeling weak as water round the knees, I scraped my key into the lock and fell through the front door.

Finding a last bit of strength from somewhere I ran up the stairs to our floor and fumbled myself in through the second lock, where, still heaving for breath – I had none left over for a shout – I took a wild-eyed look inside. All the lights were on. All the doors were open. The telly was whining to be switched off. And there was Max sprawled on the settee in this grotesque shape, her head down low and her mouth wide open. And by her side, rolled out of her reach, was not one empty bottle, but two, lying neck on neck as if they were drunk themselves.

'Christ! Max!'

I patted her face gently. I slapped it, harder. I shook her shoulders, lifted an arm, let it fall back with a dead thump.

I could feel myself turning cold. Could actually *feel* it. Was she . . . ? Could she have . . . ? I didn't even dare to think the terrible words.

But then she snored. It was like an answer; a sudden sharp snort like old ladies do in hospital.   •

'Oh, Max!'

I'd left her to get like this. I'd gone out chasing my own selfish ends while she'd got so low she'd had to drink a bottle and a half. I'd gone out to get myself straight with Wendy and left poor old Max to get in a mess like this.

I was shaking, disgusted with myself for treating her so badly. It wasn't as if I hadn't known how low she was. I twisted my face in disgust at myself. I called myself all the filthy names, told myself I deserved everything I got from anyone who wanted to dish it out. I'd crawled as low as it was possible for anyone to go. I was fouler than the dirtiest mess down Rope Street. Me, me, me! That's all I seemed to know. In a fit of loathing I wiped the back of my hand across where I'd been kissing – and suddenly knowing that wasn't enough, with a fierce, angry shout I knuckled up my fist and punched it into my face. Hit my mouth hard, as if I'd been Alfie Cox. Shocked myself with my own violence.

But even in the pain I knew it could have been much harder, if I'd had the guts to let it.

I bled like a pig. It ran all over my knuckles. My mouth filled up with it, and I careered, head back, into the bathroom. I spat, yanked at lavatory paper, and looked. My lip was split and awkward, spurting out great gobs. But it was my traitor's eyes I stared at. Get hold of that! I told myself. It'll be a good long time before you so much as *blow* a kiss again!

Clutching at the paper, moaning in my red dribble, I ran back into the sitting room and tried one-handed to get Max to her bed. But I'd reckoned without her dead, drunk weight. Without her help I wasn't going to move her anywhere.

In the end it was as much as I could do to get all of her on to the settee: and she wasn't a big woman, just awkward, with arms and legs and a neck that flopped out of all control. I dragged the eiderdown off her bed and wrapped it round her, I cleared the bottles and switched off all except one of the lights. Everything one-handed. At last there was no more I could do but stand and stare at her in her sad, dead state.

And the wet on my face as I stood there was tears as well as blood. What sort of rotten life was it, I asked myself, that changed a person from being like Wendy, on her settee, to being like Max on hers? It had all gone wrong for her; she'd been deserted by everyone till the only drop of comfort she could find was in a bottle of drink. Not even her own son cared . . .

I swore again, called God all the names, and said I was sorry to my mum. And then I got down on my knees and hugged her: I got my arms as far round her dead weight as I could, more eiderdown than Max, and I gave her the tightest squeeze in the world.

After a long time I went to clean up my mouth. But even before I came face to face with myself, I knew what I was going to stand there and tell the mirror. I'd known it as soon as I'd started that panicky run home from Wendy's.

I *was* going to find the Big Fellow. On the quiet, because it was going to have to be that way, but *certainly*. He had to sort this out for Max whether she liked it or not, because I wasn't up to it. Wendy was right about that. Her worry about me was a nice bonus, but that wasn't what was vital. What was vital was Max, lying there in her addled brain: because it suddenly seemed crystal clear that for her it could well be a matter of life and death before long.

While she was asleep I dug into the box file marked 'Private' and found the address in Richmond of the Big Fellow's agents. I wrote the phone number on a piece of paper and tucked it into my wallet, slid it under my pillow and flattened it in the dark while my legs kicked all over the bed and my brain tried to plan. The lip started throbbing like hell, and the last thing I expected to do was sleep. But in the morning I was staggered to find I'd gone off for a couple of hours at least, and what was more, a plan was beginning to form in my brain like an answer about to be posted in a pigeon hole. They were right, the psychologists.

Sleeping on something did help you to come up with solutions. Now I'd got the outline of one, and I was delighted to find that all that was needed was the detail filling in – and the final carrying-out of course!

I sat up. I felt better. Doing something about things – even thinking about telling a load of lies and being deceitful – was a fantastic cure for that terrible feeling of guilt. It even let me see Max and Wendy as two different problems: how one of them being treated badly wasn't the other one's fault – but mine.

I'd forgotten about my face, though. I'd got so used to the throbbing I'd stopped thinking about the look of it. So when I took a cup of tea into Max the question came out of the blue like another punch. While I was expecting, 'What the hell am I doing in here?' I got, 'Who the hell's been hitting you?'

'Oh, some stupid lamp post. Doing too much talking!'

'The lamp post?'

'No – me. Walked into it, not looking, didn't I?' It was the best I could come up with on the spur of the moment.

'Come off it, Kevin. You've been in a fight.'

'No, I haven't! Honest. Anyway, how are you?'

She looked down at herself lying there as if her arms and legs were someone else's: as if she needed to check how she was. She blinked round at the room that wasn't her bedroom, and she began to remember the night before. Suddenly, her arm shot out and she gripped my wrist hard. 'Kevin! *I* didn't . . . ?'

'No, love. I told you, it was a stupid lamp post. Good God!' What devils were chasing round in her head, then?

She laughed, but it hurt her head. She lay back. She swore . . . and she cried; and as I knelt down next to her with her tea I started to cry as well. Just seeing her in her misery was a pathetic sight. No one ever wants to see their mother as low as that. I could only be thankful I'd dreamt up a way of doing something about it.

Even so, it didn't stop me feeling bad about using her crying to get my plan going. In the middle of it all, as she shifted about on the settee for bits of tissue, I got hold of my most normal voice and put my big lie to her.

'Listen, Max – Nick was wondering. You know the week after next is half term?'

87

She sniffed and took a sip from her cup. 'Is it, Kev? I've lost track of time.'

'Well, you know these beach profiles we've got to do for geography? I think I told you; down at Seaford. We brought letters home last term.'

I let it out carefully, the old soft touch, but my eyes as sharp as needles for the first sign of a suspicious look.

'Yes, I know.' Not suspicious, but more alert now, pushing the hair out of her eyes. Doing her duty. Anything to do with my education seemed to sit her up.

'I thought I'd stay down for a couple of extra days with Nick while he gets his geology field study done. Be good practice for me, in case I decide to do that option . . .'

It was all a pack of lies. If you said *schist* to Nick he'd think you were swearing. But I did need to find an extra two days to do what I wanted: and turning up back home on the Thursday instead of the Tuesday would just suit me fine.

'If you help him I hope he'll give you a hand.' She'd got Nick taped.

'Yeah, but it's more the other way round. See, I'll learn how to go about it from watching him. I won't make the same mistakes, then . . .'

It was weird, but I was almost beginning to believe all this myself. In my mind's eye I could actually see me down there with a little geologist's hammer in my kit.

She wiped a shaky hand across her forehead: she had to have the mother and father of all headaches.

'How long extra will it take?'

'I said, couple of days, that's all. I'll be back for the second Saturday, the market . . .'

'And you're going when?'

'Er, Friday next week.'

'So you'll be away six days . . .'

It was uncanny how much she was on the ball. I'd have said a quick 'yes' to a kid of mine just to stop the sound of his voice.

'And staying where?'

'Youth Hostel. You remember; we had to join when we opted to do some practical. I've got my membership card.'

'Will they let you stay on?'

'Well, Nick reckons . . . '

I hadn't pictured it being this difficult when I'd planned it all in bed: my main worry had been finding an excuse for Nick, to keep him out of her way for those two days when we were supposed to be together. But this 'third degree' was something else. I think I could have been just on the verge of going red or sounding all guilty – I sometimes do that – when by a stroke of luck she suddenly broke out in a sweat and practically threw her cup at me before she dropped it.

'Oh, my God! I feel bad!'

I knelt down with her again, made some comforting noises and patted her damp head – while my brain raced to think up the answer to the next awkward question she'd ask when the wave passed. *How can I get in touch with you?* she'd want to know. She always had, right from school journeys with the juniors. *Sorry, you can't, but I can phone you.* (And who was going to know where my calls were really coming from?)

And then, like a camel kick in the chest it suddenly hit me. The Big Fellow could be miles away – could even be touring abroad. I'd always thought of him as being north London, Midlands: but wouldn't it just be my luck, the way things had gone, if I got all this fixed up, got myself the time, then found he was in Germany, or somewhere – and I actually had to end up staying down at Seaford on my own!

Max breathed in deeply and closed her eyes. 'All right, then. I'll put a couple of extra bits in.'

'Cheers, Max.'

'So you'd better phone Nick.'

'He knows,' I lied. 'Fixed it up last night.'

'Oh, thanks for taking me for granted.' But she wasn't in the mood to be either cross or comic. Words had to be counted out, this morning. But she did come back with, 'I only hope they haven't got lamp posts on that beach!'

Before I had to get a pretend smile out of my injured mouth, though, she suddenly pulled a strange face of her own and made a quick grab for the landing door. She pushed through it and slammed herself into the bathroom. I went into the kitchen and turned Capital on, loud. Everyone throwing-up is entitled to a bit of privacy; and especially Max, because being sick with her, like me with my punch in the face, was a big price to pay for a little bit of relief.

Over and over, all through that miserable Sunday, I went through what I'd say on the phone to Archer and Speight, the Big Fellow's theatrical agents, when I got back to London. It'd be a simple, straightforward enquiry, I decided, using the deepest voice I could get down to without sounding silly: *Excuse me, could you tell me where Freddie Flower and his All Stars are playing this week?* I mustn't give them the idea it was a son trying to find his runaway father, because they'd put the bars up at that – there had to be millions of jazz musicians who'd done a bunk. So, a straight question, like from a fan who'd lost touch, would be the thing. I definitely wouldn't say the Big Fellow's name.

The other thing worrying me was money, and I didn't know how to sort it out. That sudden scare I'd had about how far away the band might be had set me thinking I might have to go anywhere – up to the north of Scotland or out to the wilds of Wales; and even sleeping rough, that was going to cost a sight more than I could ask for a couple of nights' extra youth hostelling at Seaford. We had Saturday's takings in the flat, which God knew wouldn't be much, and I had a few pounds pocket money I'd put by: but what I'd really need would be my Post Office book – and that was something I'd have to get off Max. It hadn't been in the box file marked 'Private'.

Otherwise, the plan was plain sailing. Well, fairly! Pack a few things in a sports hold-all – none of that jolly rucksack stuff for what I was going to do on my own – leave the others in London (with a good excuse for Nick – perhaps even tell him the truth), then shoot over to Holland Park Hostel for the night. If it's too late to phone Archer and Speight by the time I get there, I do it next morning: dive into a call box with plenty of change, find out where the Big Fellow is, and make tracks. By coach if I can, train if I have to, and keep hitch-hiking for desperation stakes. Nothing too difficult: a simple plan, clear and straightforward, and providing the Big Fellow was in the country, one with a fair chance of success.

I began to move about a bit lighter; but Max was padding around carefully like someone who's had an operation, aware all the time of how far she was from the bathroom. Neither of us wanted much to eat, and the whole day had that flat feel of being in-between a couple of big events. Only the money really bothered me. Even Wendy had been shoved to the back of my mind, someone to think about when I had time: but at least she wasn't a worry any more.

In the end I screwed up the guts to ask Max about cash. It was late in the afternoon, just before the lights went on, when my lying face was in a bit of shadow. I was pretending to work in the bedroom when I called out all casually, 'What'll I do about money, Max?'

'Well, how much do you reckon you'll need?'

Something like fifty to be on the safe side was what I really thought: but it sounded tons too much to ask for to go down to Seaford, even with an extra couple of days. 'I don't know. What d'you reckon?'

'Take enough. You can always bring it back. You've got a money belt.'

'I'm not sure what Nick's taking . . . ' I'd never make a con man. I got too embarrassed.

'Take thirty, and go careful.'

'OK. I'll get it out of my Post Office.' That's what I wanted. The book with me, in my bag for emergencies.

'No, I've got three tens here. You'll need your book when you go to college.'

She never let go her grip on my future. Thirty! God! With the normal Seaford money to pay out and the little I'd got besides, I was just going to have to hope the Big Fellow was somewhere pretty close to London.

But I was set. All right, money was tight, but I'd already got over the biggest hurdle, bought the time to go. That, and the excuse. Now it was down to luck – and the old firm of Archer and Speight.

It's hard to describe how Max was in that week before I went to Seaford. Once the worst of that Saturday night session was over, all I could find to feel about her was that she was *different*. She was up one minute and down the next. Perhaps my knowing I was going to do something to help her made me want to keep her as she was, not to see any improvement before I made it, sort of thing; but I think I tried to be objective. I looked for her drinking; I noticed it at the time it happened; but there was a new, abnormal, energetic ultra-efficiency that seemed to go with it, although not for long at a time – and I couldn't tell whether that was a reaction to the Bacardi, part of a drinker's pattern, or some other devil driving her. I really didn't know, and I ended up more worried than ever.

And Wendy I deliberately didn't see. I phoned her a couple of times, kept in touch, told her it'd be ten or twelve days before I saw her, but that I *was* doing what she'd suggested. I still felt guilty, and that could well have been part of why I kept away: to be perfectly honest, though, it had to be the lip. It was swollen up on both sides of a deep split – really ugly – and it seemed to want to heal like the crack between the bath and the wall. So I didn't tell her about that: although I took a lot of stick about the mouth at school. 'Take care,' she said, when I told her I was going down to Seaford. 'Don't go and get yourself drowned.' Bad as things were, I decided I definitely wasn't going to do that . . .

I eventually left the flat about five o'clock on the Friday evening. Sorry to leave Max, sad not to see Wendy for so long, delighted to miss a Saturday of Alfie Cox. Ready for anything, I wore my body-warmer, a duffel coat and my thick-soled boots as I headed off for Nick's. Max shouted after me, 'You sure you'll be all right?' and I swung my sports bag round me like throwing the hammer as a sort of 'course-I-will answer. I waved like someone off to make his fortune or sell the family cow: but inside I felt a lot more like the kid with a beanstalk to climb. So much could go wrong. The Richmond agents could be closed, or engaged every time I rang; they could refuse to tell me what I wanted to know, for some reason; or they could answer all cheerfully and tell me the Big Fellow was completely out of reach. And then what would I do? God, failure at this end didn't even bear thinking about. Failure with the Big Fellow, once I'd found him, would at least mean the problem had been passed on to where it really belonged. But not to get to him with it would definitely have me hitting my head against the wall. The Archer and Speight phone call, then, would be crucial when I got back – enough to get me dreaming about it: a nightmare of finding phone boxes vandalized, having the wrong number, then hearing the line go dead when I was about to get an answer. It was horrible, and I only shook it off with the thought that at least I had a few days to relax before I came to grips with it.

And Seaford was brilliant. I'd forgotten how much I enjoyed that sort of thing: Nick, and me, and a couple of kids from our set who could always be relied on for a laugh: eight to a room in double bunks, with just what I needed, no privacy for thinking personal thoughts – and no energy, especially after a day in the open air at Cuckmere Haven, measuring the slope of the beach, throwing stones at one another, and trekking two miles back up the flood plain to the hostel. Every night there were rounds of jokes, the usual scarey stories, and before we realized no one was listening, we were all sound asleep.

I can't be sure about it, but I've got a strong idea I wouldn't have got through what was coming without that chance to be normal for a week. Like going back two years to before the family split, Seaford was a good reminder of what ordinary life could be like. Catch phrases, running jokes, and a huge attention to bowels. Even my lip didn't seem to hurt so much.

Just now and then, on that long walk down to the sea, I'd wonder how Max was: and then we saw a group of Girl Guides off to see the Long Man carved in the chalk; a smug, warm glow at knowing Wendy came over me, and I didn't howl with the rest of the lads. But otherwise it was the complete break holiday firms go on about; and when Tuesday came I packed up my gear with the slowest hands around. It was over for all of us, but it was especially over for me, because once more my life was moving me out of this age group, and leaving it so abruptly was going to be a terrible wrench.

Not only that, I'd got Wednesday and Thursday ahead, the search for the Big Fellow – and the sort of uncertainty I had to face was in even bigger contrast to the hot dinners at home the other lot were going back to.

I told Nick. On the train up from Brighton I got him on his own and said I was chasing off somewhere to find my father. Well, I had to. I couldn't have him getting on the phone to speak to me when we were still supposed to be down at Seaford together. He took it well: went all stiff-faced and responsible, and looked at me as if he was seeing a new man: but he said he'd do his best to keep his head down – and I knew he would, even if the rest of Thames Reach did find out about it afterwards.

None of the others questioned why I should shoot off in a different direction at Victoria. In a hurry to get home, off they went on the tube to Charing Cross; while I humped my bag in the opposite direction, towards the Youth Hostel in Holland Park. I got there around seven – much too late to phone Archer and Speight – booked in, had a meal, and feeling as lonely as hell to the nostalgic twang of an Australian's guitar, laid on my bed and eventually went to sleep.

But it was no one else's fault but mine that I didn't get up as early as I should have on the Thursday. I should have booked a call, because for ten days I'd known that on this morning I had to ring Archer and Speight as soon as they started picking up their phone. And yet when the day came the accumulation of bracing sea air, miles of walking, and an Australian who'd sung himself out the night before had me dead to the world late enough for even the warden to begin to wonder about me.

'Come on, Camper, out by ten, you know the rules. You getting up or do I slide you out that window?' He was joking, pleasant; but I could see his eyes going all over for a bag of glue, or something.

I rushed a wash and raced a breakfast, proved myself normal with a few semi-intelligent words before I booked out, and threw myself down the hill into the Thursday morning traffic. Now to find a telephone and a railway station, quick! But even as I was thinking of crossing the busy main road to a kiosk, along came a bus for Charing Cross, and it seemed very clear what I should do. Get on it. Go for the familiar, what you know, I told myself. Charing Cross was *our* station, served the south east, it seemed only sense to go for it.

I ran for the bus and swung on up the stairs into the smoke, where I wouldn't be disturbed by all the ons and offs.

'Must be the 'oliday, no bloody kids for a change,' one plastic briefcase said to another.

I pushed my sports bag between my feet and slumped in the

seat, putting on that bored look commuters get. I'd be doing a lot of pretending in the next couple of days, I reckoned, being on my own: might as well get used to it. I found a *Mirror* and shut myself off from any chance of talking to the briefcases by hiding behind it and getting stuck into the football. Almost at once my split lip started playing up again: it's amazing how long it takes a lip to heal, it must be all the use a mouth gets: but this was due to all that smoke, or it could have been reading about yet another battle down at the Albion, a bloody cup game which they'd drawn with Leeds on Monday night. As usual, Thames Reach had got as much space on page two, covering the court appearances, as they did at the back; and I did a big tut-tut like any peaceful passenger would.

It took us so long to get to Trafalgar Square I read the paper twice, even all the Women's Page and the stupid letters people write, and I started feeling sorry I'd ever caught the bus; but at long last there was Nelson covered in pigeons. A lot later than I'd wanted. I ran into Charing Cross station. But a quick look told me there was no way the telephones in there would do. They were those open things where the designer was the only one who thought you could hear what people were saying at the other end. I'd had experience of them before. So I hurried on: and it was a row of phones with doors, down in the Underground, that I chose in the end. And by then it was ten o'clock. The time was getting on! But at least it was late enough for Archer and Speight to be open.

Right! This was it, then! After all that time, at last the moment had come. Suddenly, my throat felt tight, as if I'd put on one of my old school shirts. My fingers trembled as I rested the coins on the cold equipment.

I dialled the number.

The connections chewed and swallowed the way they do, taking a life-time over it. And then a million miles away I heard a faint, snobby ring.

'Archer and Speight,' came a woman's voice. I pushed in the first coin while the beeps went mad. '*Hello*, Archer and Speight.'

'Oh, er, hello.' My voice was higher than I'd practised it. 'Are you the, er, the people who do Freddie Flower's All Star Band?'

'We represent Freddie Flower's All Stars, yes. Do you want *bookings* or *press*?'

'Bookings, I think . . . '

'Are you a booker?'

The money fell and the bleeps cut in again. God, that hadn't lasted long. How far away was Richmond? I pushed in the next coin.

'Hello?'

'Yes, Archer and Speight. You say you want *bookings*?'

'I'm not sure. See, I'm a . . . er, like . . . a fan. I go to see them sometimes. I just wanted to know where they are this week . . .' Hell, I hadn't sounded nearly as smooth as I'd wanted. Really rough, in fact!

'Hold the line.' Still the upper class drawl. I supposed she had to be used to dealing with all sorts: but I could picture her, hard hair and long fingernails, saying *Hold the line* in her sleep.

The money fell again and I had a real job getting the next coin in. I was all fumbles. Hurry up, woman! I hadn't realized you got so little time.

The wait was long enough to roll me over inside. What was she going to tell me? Was I in with a chance, or was the whole idea some horrible mistake? Was I going to have to call this off and lose myself somewhere for a day and a half? End up back in Thames Reach having to face Alfie Cox on my own? Leave Max to solve her problems with a bottle? Or were things going to go my way for a change? They say your life flashes past in front of you just before you drown. Well, that's nothing to what your problems do to you when you're waiting on the phone for an answer like that. At least when you're drowning you're past caring.

'Hello, caller? Now, Freddie Flower's All Stars,' she said, 'are . . . at . . . Steelton Polytechnic Hall tonight: then it's, oh, session work for a few days . . . and their next public engagement is . . . on . . . Saturday the twelfth at the Glasgow Civic Centre, and Monday and Tuesday, fourteenth and fifteenth at the Paisley Halls. Is that what you want, caller?'

'Yes . . . er . . . got that, thank you very much.'

'Glad to have been of help.' And the line went dead, a second before the last coin dropped.

Well, she'd turned up trumps after all. So, what was that? Steelton tonight. Glasgow on Saturday, then Paisley. Well, where the hell was that? And where exactly was Steelton, for that matter? Up north, somewhere, but I'd have to find a map . . . I pushed out of the box. And me doing geography! Might take it at 'A' level! What the hell use were beach studies when you didn't even know where a big city was?

I stood staring at an Underground map just to look about my business. No way could I afford to be questioned now. The band's dates meant I had to get to Steelton tonight, because I definitely couldn't go missing till Saturday – not on the Seaford excuse, even if I'd had the fare to Scotland.

But at least the band was in the country. I had to be grateful for that. At least it was *possible* to get to them. It was just that time was running so bloody short already . . .

I lugged at my bag and ran out of the Underground, up the short escalator two at a time to the main-line station. I queued impatiently while an old lady had to be helpful and find the right money. Then my turn came.

'Could you tell me, how much is a return to Steelton?'

'Trains for Steelton don't go from here.' He stared at the man behind me.

'I know they don't, but how much . . . ?'

'Enquiries.' He turned his head. 'Third window,' and switched me off again.

I went through the same routine there.

'Return to Steelton?' He tapped something on to a computer keyboard and stared at a screen I couldn't see. 'Twenty-four pounds seventy.'

'Jesus Christ!'

'Be the same for him!'

I left his wit on the glass and dragged my bag away. Nearly twenty-five pounds! Which meant, after what I'd had to spend already on the Seaford trip, that if I went by rail the only thing I could do was go single and bank on finding the Big Fellow at the other end. But what if I didn't find him? What if Steelton turned out to be a hard place to find your way about? What if the woman at Archer and Speight had got it wrong? I had to be able to get back home by Thursday, even if it was the biggest shambles going: *especially* if it was that. The last thing I could risk was being found out doing this if I failed.

I'd coach it, then. Coaches were cheaper, weren't they? I could run to a return on the coach. They took longer, but then hitch-hiking could take a life-time probably; see me still on the edge of London at six. And I had to be at Steelton Polytechnic Hall before the concert finished or my chances of finding the Big Fellow could be pretty thin.

But the bus to Victoria Coach Station seemed to take up the rest of the morning. I've never felt so frustrated in my life. I could *feel* an ulcer growing down inside me. Stop, start, stop, start down Whitehall, round the statue of Winston Churchill, a look at the galloping clock up Big Ben, down past the Abbey: it was all traffic lights and a million passengers waiting to get on and off. The day was runing away through my fingers.

At last we pulled up opposite and I ran into Victoria Coach Station with my bag doing a great tripping job between my legs. It was eleven o'clock by then.

The place was like the sort of garage you come across on holiday: lines of coaches in unusual colours using bays instead of bus stops, a lot of white steering wheels instead of black, and roller blinds saying *Relief*. People darted about all round the coaches, the drivers stowed the luggage, and an inspector stood in the middle shouting things like, 'Any more for Bristol?' It wasn't a bit like the railways; there was no big deal about any of the passengers. I just felt as if I'd gone back a hundred years, into the olden days of the stage coach. And I didn't mind that a bit, as long as they'd got the Steelton run down to a reasonable time.

There's no big deal, but there's a big difference in the fares. That was my first surprise. I queued up at the ticket counter and asked for a return to Steelton. 'I'm going there today, and coming back tomorrow,' I said, to make everything as clear as I could.

I was impressed. The girl behind the window actually looked at me. Well, stared at my mouth. 'You a student?' she asked with a frown.

'That's right.' That's what it said on my passport: though I couldn't think what business that was of hers.

'Service 302,' she told me, writing out the ticket. 'Eight pounds, please.'

Eight! Strewth! That was some improvement on nearly twenty-five. That meant, if I didn't find the Big Fellow at least I could get a bed for the night and go on looking in the morning. This hadn't been half a bad move, coming for the coach. I gave her one of the tens, but she kept her hand held out for more. 'I've given you ten,' I told her. 'You said it was eight.'

'Student card,' she sighed. 'Come on, you know that – if you're supposed to be a student . . . '

'Eh? I . . . Oh, I haven't got one of them . . . '

'I asked you "Student?" didn't I?'

They get ratty so quickly, people behind windows. Perhaps it's the being caged-up does it. All impatiently, she crossed out bits of the ticket. 'That's fourteen-fifty, then. Four-fifty to pay.'

My heart sank. Having heard the price they were happy to take students for, I begrudged handing over the extra money. 'So how much does a student card cost?' I asked her.

'You can't just buy one. Ask at your college.'

'Oh.'

I slid my bag to the side with my foot and counted what I had left. Already, I'd spent fifteen-fifty today. With the money I still had from Seaford that left me with a bit over eight. Not a lot to go careering off to the north of England with . . .

But, good luck! There was nothing I could do about that. The big thing now was to get away. I could worry some more once the coach wheels were turning. I ran to the bay for Steelton, and I found the coach with 302 on the front. The driver was bending into the boot, pushing cases right to the back with a broom.

'This the coach for Steelton?' I asked him, to be on the safe side. He straightened up from the boot as if it was a clever trick he did, making his wavy grey hair miss the over-hanging door by a centimetre.

He looked down at my sports bag, just a glance at first, then a longer look – a double-take. Surely to God he'd put a sports bag in with those scruffy cases.

'You on your own?'

'Yes.' I stood up taller. He couldn't refuse to take me on account of my age, could he? 'I paid full fare,' I told him.

'I don't doubt it, lad. Hey up, you'd best get in, then, I'm late off as it is.'

I didn't like his frown, wouldn't have bothered him any more, but I badly needed to know something else. 'What time do we get to Steelton?'

'Four o'clock, lad. If I don't get held up by you an' get away quick.'

He'd be home for tea, then, I thought – judging by his accent. *Hovis* country. But it was good news for me. Getting in at four o'clock would give me all the time in the world to find the Polytechnic Hall and get to the Big Fellow before he went on. Give him some time to be thinking about the arrangements he'd need to make.

I left my hold-all and ran round into the coach, found a window seat. I showed Hovis my ticket when he came for it – he'd still got that miserable frown for me, but a smile and 'Ta, love,' for the old girls who might tip him – and with the coach still half-full he hissed the door shut, and we were away. Thank God for that! I thought. Properly off at last. But it was a really weird feeling, pulling out of London going north when as far as anybody else in the world knew I was down south. I don't think I'd ever been where no one could get hold of me before.

I leant my head against the window, closed my eyes and tried to relax a bit. It was going all right now, I told myself. I was definitely doing the right thing. Wendy had helped me to make up my mind, but it was the state Max was in that had *convinced* me. It had been staring both of us in the face for weeks. Neither of us needed an 'A' level in Economics to know that her business was on the slide. It had never been a big money-spinner, but the last couple of weeks we'd been lucky even to *see* any. Take the man who'd turned up on Saturday for a passport holder he'd ordered: been promised. It hadn't been ready, and he'd gone away with that look on his face that said he definitely wouldn't bother coming back. And being fair, with Max all uncertain about where she stood, who could blame her for letting the heart go out of it all? Or who could blame me if the heart had gone out of my fight with the Coxes now I'd turned it into a matter of life and death? No, whether Max wanted it or not, we both needed the Big Fellow to help us out:

just a couple of days of his time, then he could go back to his life on the road: no skin off his nose. I was definitely doing the right thing. The *only* thing. And surely to God he'd come! There wasn't any doubt about that, was there?

I opened my eyes, caught another nasty look from Hovis in the interior mirror, and closed them again. I shifted down in the double seat I'd got to myself and tried to get comfortable for a sleep. But sleep never comes to order, not even when you're dog-tired. I was much too restless. And I had too much seat. What I really needed was someone there with me; someone to talk to who was on my side, someone's head to have resting on my shoulder. Which had to be Wendy's, of course! Wendy, who knew the score between me and the Coxes now. Wendy, who I'd whispered secret things to. And suddenly I had that terrible feeling of being split down the middle again: *because* the one I wanted next to me was Wendy, and my rotten conscience told me that the only head that needed a bit of support right now was Max's. She was my first responsibility, wasn't she?

It took us the best part of an hour to get to the motorway, and then the long drone began: that steady, noisy hum that gets everybody off to sleep in the end, a couple of hours of it; till what woke us up was a sudden slowing down, indicators clicking us into the near-side lane and a run up the short slope into a services area. Hovis backed the coach into a parking space, opened the door and stood up, all important.

'We'll be twenty minutes here,' he announced, boring at me with his eyes as if I was the only one on his blessed coach. 'Don't be late back, please.'

I was more than ready for the stop, and so were the others judging by the impatient shuffling to get off. Out of curiosity I looked up and down the coach to see if anyone had the sort of bladder that'd take them all the way; but there weren't any. The coach emptied right out. I know it did, because the door was locked when they brought me back later to pick up my things.

Inside the services building it was all bleeping Space Invaders and people wandering about in a trance. A policeman walked up and down and kept an eye without actually seeming to look at anyone. I took it all in – and quickly made up my mind. I was starving hungry and I could have murdered a Coke; but who knew what sort of prices they'd charge at a place like this? So I reckoned I'd best not dip into what I'd got left here. I'd do without for once, wait till I got to Steelton; it couldn't be that long. I used the urinal, dried my hands under an air-blow, and swilled my mouth out gently at a drink fountain. Then with nothing else to do I wandered out to get back to the coach and wait for the rest. But I didn't get to take two steps outside the gents! As I shoved my hands in my pockets ready to stroll off – minding my own business and taking in what was going on around – suddenly, there was Hovis and the prowling police-man blocking my way at the Space Invaders, holding out their arms as if I was some sort of a runaway.

'This is the lad,' Hovis said. 'Y'can't see it yet-a-while, but his bag's in the boot.'

'Ah, yes.' That policeman didn't look much older than me; but he stared at me as if I'd done a murder, and when he moved his mac gave off a loud noise which had all the sound of authority.

I screwed up my face at him. So what the hell was up then? Surely to God it couldn't be Max? She'd nowhere near sus-pected I was pulling a trick, I'd stake my life on that. So what was it? Was there some mistake over the ticket. Or had they got me mixed up with some kid on the run?

'And where are you off to, lad?' The policeman wasn't looking at my eyes. It was my mouth and my beach study boots that had his attention.

'Steelton! *He* knows, for crissake!' I gave Hovis a look to kill.

'Oh, yes? Steelton, eh?' The policeman tapped his foot and went on staring, as if the combination might make me say something he really wanted to hear.

'That's right, Steelton. So what?'

'Live there, do you? Got an address you're going to?'

'No. Not yet.'

'Not yet? *Not yet?* That's a funny sort of answer, isn't it? You sure it's not Steelton on this, and then the bus to Leeds?'

'No. Steelton. Steelton Polytechnic Hall. What the hell's going on?'

'Poly-technic? Bit young for poly-technic, aren't you? I think we'll have a little look in your bag, my lad.'

'Please yourself.' I'd got nothing to hide. No tubes of glue or flick knives or porno books in there: just a shirt and socks and a pair of pants. One look and he'd soon have to say he was sorry and let me go.

He took me by the arm: a really tight grip, the sort you see the yobs getting at the football grounds but quite unnecessary for me. The Space Invaders seemed to stop bleeping, and under all those big eyes and open mouths I was walked out of the building and across the car park to the coach. God, don't some people love to see someone else in trouble?

He didn't say a thing. And neither did I till I knew what I was supposed to have done: which gave me about twenty metres in all the noise of that racing traffic to make my mind up about how much of the truth I was going to tell him: because one thing was dead certain – I couldn't tell it all. If he found that Max didn't know where I was, he'd escort me straight back to London without my feet touching – just to keep his hands clean.

The trouble is, once you start lying it's so easy to trip yourself up. Like saying you're staying in Seaford when you're going north to Steelton. You had to remember who you had to tell which lie to. The best thing, I told myself as I got to the coach, was to act a bit slow on the uptake: give myself time to think. Go over all the possibilities a couple of times before I said anything.

And I needed to, when I found out what they were thinking. Hovis unlocked the coach for the policeman to push me up inside, then he went round to the boot and came back with my hold-all.

'There it is,' he said, all proud of himself. 'I told you, it's written all over.'

I sat on the seat by the door, a big, thick frown on my face; the policeman stood in the well and took the bag from Hovis; gave me a small tingle of pleasure when he slid the door shut on the little smarm.

He looked at the bag and he looked at me. He held it up as if the photographers were there. And all of a sudden I could see what both of them were seeing; written all over it like the man said. *Thames Reach Albion*: a plastic sports bag in the local colours I'd bought to be the same as the rest of the kids at school.

'So?' I pretended with a slow look and stretched my neck forward: but now I knew what they were on about. Idiot! Why the hell hadn't I realized how close to Leeds I was going – and dumped the bag? Wasn't there a replay there tonight? A grudge match? What a berk I was not to have packed myself up into one of the million other non-football bags we had at home.

He looked down at my tough boots; he bent his spotty white face closer to my split lip.

'How d'you get that, then?'

Everything fitted in to his simple little theory.

'I walked into a lamp post.'

'Oh, yes?' His sarcastic voice said I was a rotten liar. 'Wouldn't be a lamp post wearing a Leeds United scarf, would it?'

'No!' I wanted to act slow, but I didn't have the time. People were coming back to the coach and looking in the windows – and I wanted to be off just as much as they did. 'I know what you reckon,' I told him. 'You think I'm travelling "away", don't you? Thames Reach Albion.' Everyone who could read knew that Thames Reach supporters were banned from other grounds.

'That's what the driver thinks, aye.'

'I thought there was something up with him.'

'Well, you can't blame him, can you, lad? Even the Met. police'd tumble to that! Your bag, your steel-capped boots, your split lip – and going as close as you can get taken for the match without actually travelling on a Leeds coach. If that don't add up, I don't know what does.'

I looked at him, hard. It was open and shut to him, the way it had been to Hovis. Neither of them looked further than the ends of their noses. The only reason I hadn't been stopped at Victoria was the chance it would have made Hovis late – and now he'd found a mate up here who'd sort it out without a hold-up. It was all so perfect, the way everything seemed to fall into place: so much so you'd think that very fact on its own would make them think. Did they *really* imagine anyone'd be that thick – to carry a bag with that written on it, "away"? I smiled, and hurt my lip.

'Do you reckon I'm so thick as to carry this bag up to Leeds if that's what I'm about? Up there, on my own, after Monday night? They're animals, both lots. There'll be murders up there . . . '

But he just stared at me with that policeman's look of not even really listening to what I was saying.

'All right, I'll tell you, for your information. My name's Kevin Kendall, and I really am going to Steelton, for the simple reason I'm going to hear my dad playing trumpet with Freddie Flower's band. And his name's Bill Kendall. Right? And the reason I've got a Thames Reach bag's because I happen to live there, and believe it or not, bags come in handy for putting your gear in.'

Pick the bones out of that! I thought. Which was a mistake, because being sarcastic only made him dig his heels in harder.

'Well, we can soon check that out, can't we?' He opened the door to the crowd of idiots who were stretching their necks to hear what Hovis was saying. 'Come on, we'll get on the phone. Driver, have you got this lad's ticket?'

And only then did it hit me. He was going to put me off. Make me miss the coach. But he couldn't! He couldn't let this coach go on, and leave me here in the middle of nowhere! I'd miss the Big Fellow. It'd ruin everything!

I was only grateful Wendy wasn't there when he led me off in that same criminal grip, with my bag in his other hand. I could be innocent or guilty, they just have to show they're the bosses, some policemen. Where the hell could I run to, anyway? Up the fast lane? And all those eyes as I was walked past! All the second-hand thrills the old ladies got as the naughty boy was held safe in front of them! Hovis wet his finger and picked out my ticket: gave it to the policeman while he did his best not to look at me by checking the rest and putting them away ever so carefully.

A great wave of anger suddenly rushed in and took my breath away. 'You stupid git!' I croaked at him. 'How'm I supposed to get to Steelton now?'

'Enough of that! You can get the next coach – if you're supposed to be there at all.' And the policeman pulled me away before I could aim the kick I wanted to.

Through the thick windows of the police room the traffic belting past in silence could have been on a screen, or in some other world. And Steelton really could have been a million miles away for all my chances looked of getting to the Big Fellow in time.

My bag – Hovis's precious evidence – was slung up on to a table and gone through in double-quick time. All the innocent things came out – till just as I was about to give him a good smug grin because he hadn't found a bicycle chain, the bag suddenly did unzip a very nasty surprise.

'This your telephone number? Here on the lining?'

It was: felt-tipped with a few fancy scrolls one boring evening over a year before.

I felt sick. It was a good job I hadn't had any food, because I think I'd have brought it up there and then, all over his traffic cones. Christ! I'd been thinking any check he made would be at the Steelton end – and now this man had enough to go on to phone Max back at Thames Reach. What the hell would she say to the news that I was halfway up the M1 when she thought I was down in Sussex? And on my way to one of the Big Fellow's concerts, too! She wasn't soft. She'd go spare, demand that I was sent straight home.

'There's no one in, there,' I said, a bit too strong to be convincing. 'Er, my mother's out at work all day.'

But that didn't bring the slightest slow-down in his dialling.

I don't think I've ever in my life watched a face more closely for some sign of what was going on. Any second his eyes were going to light up like a pinball machine and the crunch conversation was going to begin. His fingers tapped out some secret beat in his brain; while mine were just clenched tight with the terrible tension.

But his fingers went tapping on, verse two and a chorus, and mine started to loosen; just a bit. The phone at home was ringing and ringing . . . and a faint glimmer of hope was beginning to grow. Max was either out of the house, or she wasn't hearing the bell.

My fingers were all over the place now in a jittery dance of their own: a dead give-away which I quickly hid from him by shoving them into the pockets of my jeans.

And there they found the touch of a vital scrap of paper.

Not daring to hope too much, I pulled it out.

'You could always try this,' I told him. 'My father's agents. Archer and Speight. They can soon tell you whether I'm telling the truth.'

His eyes suddenly flickered. Please God! Had I done the trick, or had Max picked the phone up? A sudden spurt of adrenalin shot around inside.

The flicker was for my piece of paper. I suppose he needed an answer as much as I did now, with the phone not being picked up. Slowly, he put it down while he read the phone number; and then, without a word, he dialled it.

It was answered very quickly.

'Oh, er, Leicestershire police here,' he said. He didn't muck about: straight in with it. 'I've got a lad here, claims he's on his way to see his father with a band called . . . ' He looked up at me.

'Freddie Flower's All Stars.' If it was the snobby lady at the other end I put up a quick prayer that she was still prepared to be helpful.

'Yes, with, er, Freddie Flower's All Stars. A person known as Kendall . . . '

'Bill Kendall, plays lead trumpet,' I rushed in quickly.

'Apparently a Bill Kendall, love. Can you confirm he's on your books?'

He waited. He nodded. He grunted. While I sweated – waiting in a police room for the say-so that the Big Fellow still existed!

'Right. Aye. That's what the lad says, Steelton Polytechnic Hall.' He still said it as if he was writing it down. 'That's the information we have. Thanks a lot, love, ta . . . '

He stared at me as if he was suddenly telling me something new. 'This band of yours is at a Steelton venue tonight.'

'I know it is. I told you that on the coach!' I scraped back my chair, wild at being made to miss the only transport that would definitely get me there in time, and not even a 'sorry' from the man. But I couldn't push my luck too far. There were a million things he could do if he wanted to: like pulling me in for having a rusty zip on my bag, or something. Some policemen are full of little tricks like that. No – getting on fast meant saying as little as possible to rub him up the wrong way.

He stood up. 'I'll make sure you get on the next coach,' he said. 'But if I was you I'd hang my coat over the words on that bag. You're dead right, lad, there could be murders up there tonight . . . '

'What time's the next one?'

'Around five. If we haven't had a pile-up.'

'What the hell time is that going to get me there?'

He shrugged, all noise in that coat. 'I don't carry the time-tables, lad.'

Now he had his only-doing-my-job face on again. I hated those dead eyes; hoped he knew he had all those spots on his chin. And as I watched him pretending to read some of the bits of paper on the table, I saw that old familiar look about him. The Simple Saunders look: the Hovis eyes: the Old Lavender mouth. It was the ugly face of the small-time official going about his business, the look to make you feel really depressed because you saw it everywhere you went, met it all through your life.

Except I'd got one up on this policeman. With a bit of luck, I told myself, I was on my way to hear the Big Fellow play: the blues, some ragtime, watch him go out on a limb with 'You Can Have Your Cake and Eat It If You Try'. I was going to hear my father do more tonight than this bloke could rise to in a lifetime. Hear him play and hear the loud applause. So really, shouldn't I be feeling sorry?

Sorry! I almost thumped his table. No way! After being put off that coach I'd be damned if I felt sorry for anyone – except me.

Chapter Eight

I was riding shotgun on the edge of my seat, pushing the coach on over every metre as we ran into Steelton. The half past five 302 had got into the services more like twenty past six, and by the time they'd had their break and I'd got through to a thick driver about how I'd missed the other coach, it was getting on for seven when we actually pulled out into the slow lane. I'd been there so long it was hard to believe I was part of the world that moved again, finished at last with that depressing middle-of-nowhere place. What a drag of a wait! If things had been more normal I might have sat down on my heels, slipped my Hohner out of my back pocket and quietly played a few tunes to myself. As a rule time and worries seem to pass peacefully away when I do that. But my split lip had put a stop to even that little consolation: and by the time I got in the coach I was ready to bang my head against the window in frustration. Looking at my watch, I should have been in Steelton by then – round the back, letting the Big Fellow know I was there, telling him the tale. Instead of which I was two hours away, and it'd only take a mile of road works to make me miss him altogether. And then where would I be, trying to find him in a strange place? He could be in the mini van or whatever and away off out of the city in no time. I don't know why, though – somehow the second part of something always seems quicker than the first, the part after the interval or the journey home, so when Steelton started coming up on the road signs, gradually working its way up to the top of the list, I began to feel a bit more hopeful, started edging my backside towards it as if that would somehow get me there that much quicker.

Then all at once we were off the M1 and running along a clearway direct to the centre of the city. No hour of suburbs, no enormous sprawl of houses. Suddenly we were there; and it wasn't two minutes before it hit me how different it was to London; how it was all divided up so that traffic and pedest-trians never actually met: which is all very nice till you want to change from one into the other. The end result is you feel less human, less important, as you try to work out what you're supposed to do in their weird system of precincts and race tracks. No wonder places like Steelton have taxis like Thames Reach has pigeons: you almost have to call one to get you across the road.

But there I was with no money for a taxi. I was hungry, thirsty, tired, cold and in a screaming hurry: and without the cash to spare to sort any of it out.

Loud shouts of show-off chanting came from somewhere near: which could just as easily have been the National Front as the football because that was thirty miles away in Leeds: all the same, I took a chance on the cold and threw my duffel over the Thames Reach bag. I hadn't come this far to get a good kicking. But it all added to the nasty feeling of being well out of my own territory, a long way from home. It was hard to think of this different life going on all the time from choice, so far away from Thames Reach.

And what was harder still was thinking of the Big Fellow swapping what he'd had with us for night after night of feeling like this sort of stranger.

But, God, the time was getting on. Racing past. Looking round in panic I saw an inspector in the coach station who might just about know where he was.

'Could you tell me where the Polytechnic Hall is, please?'

He looked at the timetable in his hand as if the answer could be there, but he was only waving a coach away.

'Polytechnic Hall? They're all over the place, love. Do you know which one it is you're after?'

Love? I *was* on another planet.

'It's the one where Freddie Flower and the All Stars are playing.' He must have heard of a visiting band like that.

'Oh, I can't keep up with all the student hops. The top-liners go to the *Palace*. Not at the *Palace*, are they?' His frown told me he doubted it.

'No, it's definitely Steelton Polytechnic Hall.'

He looked round for someone to ask himself, but there was no one handy. 'You try the one in Barnsley Road. Service 11 bus. Get it up there, love.' He pointed away up the street, briefly, before he got to grips again with the front of another coach.

I lugged the bag to the bus stop. It was a cold, windy wait, with my eyes getting crossed, between looking up for the bus and down at my watch. Till at last the noisy green thing came – and a cheap fare it turned out to be for all the stops we had to go. For what I paid, I thought it'd be round the corner, but on and on we went, till I was starting to think the conductor had forgotten to put me off. But suddenly, there it was, a big, grey old-fashioned building stuck in the middle of a street of steel and glass: POLY HALL!

And there, outside on the wall, in a long line of day-glo posters, was the name I'd dreamt of seeing for nearly two years: FREDDIE FLOWER AND THE ALL STARS. But, like a lot of dreams, it was a disappointment: because although it was there, it was only printed small, on the bottom third of the poster under 'supported by' – holding up the real star of the evening, RADIO'S STAR DJ – PETER PRICE, HERE IN PERSON. Peter Price! The great poof! I tore the sleeve up my arm to get at the time. Nine o'clock! And them the supporting act. God alive, they could be off and finished by now!

I tripped and swore at that bloody bag as I ran for the big main doors. From somewhere deep down inside I heard cheers and claps and the usual wild screams. Who the hell was that for? The All Stars going off or Peter Price coming on? I had to know, had to get straight into the back of that hall. But, being me, as I ran into the main entrance I found my way blocked by two gorilla students sitting dangling their legs on a table halfway up the grand staircase: hard looking cases in tight red tee shirts under a sign which said, PLEASE DON'T ASK FOR CREDIT AS A SMACK IN THE TEETH OFTEN OFFENDS.

I scrambled with a hand in my jeans. 'How much to get in?'

They looked at me as if I was something I'd walked in off the pavement on a shoe.

'Got a Union card?'

'No. I'll pay full price.' So, it was the same old hassle, was it? But money didn't matter any more if the Big Fellow was on the other side of those doors.

One of them laughed at the other, but it was aimed at me. 'Everyone pays full price, son.' He was a Londoner. 'You just don't get in at all without a Union card, on account of it's a Union do.'

I threw down my Thames Reach bag, loud as I could on the marble floor. 'Oh, come on!' I shouted. 'Leave it out! My old man's in there playing lead trumpet. I've come all the way from the other side of London to see him.'

'Then you're too late, my son. Just gone off, your little lot.' He didn't budge from blocking my way. I stared at his hard, couldn't-care face. It was unbelievable. Obviously he came from another part of London to me – or it could just have been another street. It's crazy how hard some people try to find the differences.

But the other one, a Welshman, tried to be a bit more helpful. 'Get yourself round the back doors, boy. Catch 'em as they go out.'

I didn't stop to thank him. I scooped up my bag and legged it out the way I'd come in. I grazed all down my arm on the old grey wall, and I didn't feel a thing as I raced for the back doors – all arms, legs, flappy coat and awkward bag.

And I suddenly stopped as I ran round the last sooty corner and almost into the back of a battered old blue Transit with its doors wide open.

I leant against the wall to get my breath back as a slight scruffy man carrying a big drum case came staggering out to the van and heaved it up into the back. He looked as if he could have done with a hand, but I was all in.

'Excuse me,' I said, 'is this Freddie Flower's All Stars?'

He went on shoving in the drum as far as it would go. Then he turned round to face me. He blinked a couple of times, and I stared at the tired face.

It was my dad.

There was just that moment, that fraction of an instant when you could see his brain trying to place me. Well, you change a lot in eighteen months at my age. And then he knew.

'*Kevin!*'

He nearly broke my back with his hug. A year and a half of it. He pinned me and shook me and roughed my face with his bony chin: he groaned and cried and wouldn't let go: and I stood and swayed off balance, and just trusted him to keep me up.

The Big Fellow! I was crying, too, with my head above the shoulder that had carried me high round the park. I couldn't even say his name: it was only a grizzle coming from me.

'Put her down, Bill!' Someone had come up behind us and was trying to move him to one side: but the someone suddenly stopped and put a heavy case on the pavement. There was a banging of a door, and the sound of loud voices being shushed, and deep conversation. But I heard all that as if it was going on in another world: because the real world was here: what I was gripping hold of with my own two hands.

It didn't take him more than five minutes to get us to a wine bar: after a quick word with someone at the hall, he gripped my arm and hurried us under three roads and a precinct, and before I knew where I was he was pushing at the paint on a glass door.

'This'll be all pie crust and brown plates,' he said. 'but at least you can hear yourself talk in here.'

'Long as it's food,' I told him. 'I'll have about eight of everything!'

A girl in a long skirt and one of those home-made hair styles took us to a table close to the bar; but the Big Fellow didn't like it. He found the table he wanted in a quiet corner and sat us down there. I felt myself unwinding inside. Just over that, it felt good to be with someone who got what they wanted for once. And it makes a nice change, not having to stand on your own two feet.

As he turned his head to talk to her I took a quick look at him in the light. It was weird, doing that. It was like seeing someone you knew from a lot of old films suddenly showing up in a new one: when you've got him in your mind as the young hero and he suddenly turns up as an old character. Of course, I must have grown up a bit and changed myself since I'd seen him – and they say you grow quickest at my age – but he'd easily altered as much as me. Although eyes don't change so much: and it was a real shock to see something familiar looking out of that stranger's face – where lines had started joining up the features and hairs grew from places they wouldn't have dared to grow from before. Just like waking yourself up from a dream you're not pleased with, I felt like closing my eyes and trying again. All the same – and forget the brown stains on his teeth – his eyes were the same old blue, just ever so slightly paler, and he had the same eye-lashes, long and light with faint lines under the rims that looked like make-up. Actor's eyes. Musician's eyes. *Performer's* eyes. Even in his cracked leather top and worn-white jeans you couldn't mistake the man who'd not long come off a stage.

There was no asking me about the food. 'We'll both have your pork pie, plenty of it, love, and salad and a bit of bread; with a Coke for the boy and a glass of red wine for me.' But he didn't need to ask. At the sound of it my inside started up like a washing machine. I could put paid to anything he called for.

And with the ordering out of the way, he folded his arms and stared at me across the table.

'So what the devil are you doing up here? It's not Max, is it? She's all right, is she?'

'Yeah, she's all right. Only – '

'What's up then, Kevin? And what the hell's happened to your lip? You're not in bother, are you? Not a gang thing, is it?'

'No . . .'

I picked at the brown sugar with my fingers. I rubbed at the puckered table cloth. Where on earth did you begin to fill in on a lost eighteen months? How quickly could you get to the point? I made my mind up to go for it direct. After all, he hadn't carefully got us in the mood for the crisis he'd caused, had he? And he'd seemed to ignore the possibility that I might simply have wanted to see my father again.

'This – ' I fingered my split lip and I watched him touch his own, the way people do – 'this isn't anything. Argument with a lamp post in Rope Street, that's all. What's really up is the licence on the market stall. It's run out and it's got to be renewed.'

'Oh? Well, how much is that?'

'That's just it. It's not *how much*. It's *who*. See, it's the third

114

year and Max isn't allowed to renew it without a new signature from you. It's still in your name, see? So if it isn't you who takes it out again, it's a new application. Even Max is a new application: and this time anyone could get it if you don't want it.'

'Oh, I see. Least, I think I do. And *does* anyone else want it?'

'You're joking! Only the Coxes.'

'The Coxes? Who are they when they're at home?'

I'd forgotten that he might not know. I'd lived with the Coxes so long it seemed as if I'd been up against them for ever. 'Next door. Fancy goods. You know, shouting the odds sort of stuff. They want us out like mad, so's they can expand, and I'll tell you, they don't exactly make life easy . . . '

It was incredible. After all the aggravation I'd had, after all those miserable mornings when I'd wanted him around, here I was making the Coxes sound like nothing worse than a couple of difficult kids in the first year. As it happened, I didn't have to worry about whether to tell him more about the Coxes just then because the food came – a big slice of pork pie with egg in that didn't touch the sides as it went down. For a few minutes I couldn't think of anything else in the world except those juicy mouthfuls. But while I was practically swallowing the plate whole, the Big Fellow was just forking his food about and picking at his questions.

'Going well, is it, the stall?'

'Not bad.'

'Your mum's . . . enjoying it?'

'All right.'

'She *wants* to keep it on, then?'

I nodded.

'And they reckon her name's not good enough without mine?'

'Useless. Twice, they've told her that. She's got just the same chance as anyone else who wants it.'

'But if I sign it, she'll get it?'

'Yeah. Well, *you'll* get it, for the next three years. You've still got first option, or something.'

He dangled a little ring of onion on his fork while he thought, holding it in front of his mouth as if he was making up his mind about it.

'And she asked you to come and find me, have a word about it?'

Quickly, I put in another big mouthful and slid the Coke my way. I chewed and swallowed slowly while I tried to think what to say.

'Well, not in so many words, she didn't *tell* me to come. But she didn't, sort of, *stop* me, either . . . ' I was lying, but I wasn't actually telling a lie. I was just not telling him all the truth – her suddenly going downhill and the drinking stuff. I knew I could have done: it would have helped to persuade him, no doubt about that; but for some funny reason I just didn't want him to do anything out of pity. That wouldn't be fair to her. I wanted him to *want* to do it, even if it cost him something to himself.

Especially if it cost him something to himself!

'How's she been, Kev? She's certainly looking all right, eh?'

'Yeah, not too bad.' I dropped my fork and stared back at him. How the hell did he know what she was looking like?

He smiled, but sadly. 'We come down south now and then. I had a wander round Thames Reach a couple of months back. Saw her in one of the shops . . . '

It was one of the saddest things I'd ever heard.

'Where do you live, then?'

'Birmingham. Got a room there. Pretty handy, like, for getting about.'

I shut my mouth: the food, the drink and the questions had all gone. Besides, I wasn't too sure I could trust my voice any more: this was all getting too much.

'So,' he said, 'it's a bed for the night for you – and what sounds like plenty to sleep on for me.' The onion finally dropped from his fork as he pushed first his plate then his chair away, and got up. And once again I was surprised by how much smaller he looked on the other side of this table than he had at home. He wasn't really the Big Fellow any more, I thought: not in that sense.

Then he nearly had the whole thing over as he threw his arm round me and bear-hugged me to him.

'It's good to see you, Kev!'

'And you – ' I hugged him back.

116

'Bill. Call me Bill . . .'

'Yeah. Bill.' I croaked. But somehow 'Bill' didn't sound right: not the way 'Max' did. He'd always been 'Dad' to his face and the 'Big Fellow' in my head. So I shut my mouth and let the hugging say it for me.

The Carlton wasn't really much more than an ordinary house with little signs and fire doors, but it was the hotel where all the others were staying that night and it was a handy place for the Big Fellow to find me a bed. In the sitting room there was an alcove just about big enough for a telly at home; but Mrs Pearce, the owner, had squeezed a bar in there – and that's where she was when we went in, laughing and filling up glasses for three men in white shirts and blue bow ties, members of the All Stars band. I recognized Freddie Flower from the old days, but none of the others rang any bells.

I nodded to him, a bit nervous – because something wasn't quite right in there – and sharp-eyed Mrs Pearce caught me out.

'Love-a-duck, Sunshine, cheer up! You've found old Bill, haven't you?'

News travels fast round a small band. I nodded and gave her my shy look.

'So, it's a Bell's for Bill, and – '

'A cider, please.'

' – And a cider for our young man. And don't you worry, love,' she winked at me, 'I've got a camp bed for you upstairs. Mrs Pearce won't turf you out in the cold!'

She was one of those cheerful women, a bit like my Essex gran who'd really spoil me if ever she got to see me: and I could just see all this lot telling her their troubles and handing round the family colour prints.

'You can tell we stay here quite a bit,' the Big Fellow told me – quietly, as if it was a business secret. 'Come over in this corner . . .'

But even in the corner there was nowhere private enough to talk – not the sort of talk we needed to have. Three men in jumpers were going on about double-glazing sales, sitting about as far away as you'd rest your glass, and across the room the All Stars band was getting noisier and noisier; taking the rise, mostly, out of the DJ who'd topped their bill. 'A right twonk,' one of them said, 'thought a middle-eight was an extra crew in the Boat Race!'

Bill didn't join in, though: not the talk and not the laughing. He just sat, feet apart, hands dangling in front of him, like someone sitting in the hospital who isn't sure whether he's with the doctors or the porters.

There was such a lot I wanted to ask him. What *was* life like for him? Was it what he'd wanted when he upped and off? Did he still play the blues – 'Chimes', 'Beal Street', 'Mood Indigo' – the way that always got the feet tapping and the eyes sparkling back at the Empress? Did he still remember what it used to be like when we went on the trips together? When we went for our games round the park? And, above all, was he going to do what I'd come to ask him?

'Well, Bill?' Freddie Flower came over – and when the Big Fellow shifted his seat and looked awkward I thought he was going to broach the subject of a few days' leave. But no such luck. Before he could say anything, Mrs Pearce slid in to bring our drinks and ruffle my hair, and the moment had passed.

'Well, chick-a-biddy,' she said, 'you're certainly a chip off the old block.' She stood smiling all satisfied at the two of us as if she'd been the one to bring us together. 'You've come a long way, have you?'

'Yes, that's right.' You had to be polite, humouring: she was putting herself out for us. 'But thanks to some stupid coach driver I missed seeing him play tonight.'

'Who, our Freddie? Oh, he'll give you a tune now, won't you love? Give us all one. Have a party, eh?' She lifted the edge of her skirt and twirled a foot.

'Actually, I meant my dad . . .'

'Your dad?' She was looking very dense at me. And he was getting up, making a funny noise in his throat. 'But your dad doesn't play. He's the driver, aren't you, love? Here, whatever have you been telling your boy?'

He just made this noise: I stared at his white face: and it might have been the journey, or the pork pie I'd bolted, or the shock, but suddenly nothing in the world could stop me spewing a whole lung-full of cider all over the swirly pattern on the carpet. Cider, and then, pie. Like throwing back at someone everything I'd ever swallowed.

Chapter Nine

'I'd have given quids for you not to know,' he said.

The coach was heading back south against the wind, and I had my head pressed against the window, thinking about Wendy.

'Yeah?'

That evening, at her house, all close, when we'd sort of fitted together as if that was the way we'd been made, seemed about the only good thing to have happened to me for years. Everything else, and you could include this so-called victory – bringing him back to sort out the business – had just *had* to go wrong, hadn't it?

So the Big Fellow didn't play lead trumpet after all! Another floorboard collapsing under Kevin Kendall. I'd had no sleep with the news of that. Not that I could even begin to get to grips with it. It was too big. What I'd thought the guy was all about just hadn't been true. The way I'd seen him for eighteen months, the man who'd run off and left us because he was the artist, the performer, doing his own thing because he had to, had been wrong all the time. There I'd been, seeing him as the man we'd lost so's he could be a star, standing in the front line, getting all the applause – while all the time he'd only been the driver for the outfit.

And what had really kept me turning on that hard canvas all the night, was where did that leave Max and me now? Being left because he had to give every minute to his music, well, that was one thing: you could just about bring yourself to tell anyone about that: but being thrown-over for the thrill of him being an odd-job driver was something else again. That was just being left – for the sake of it.

'Soon as I knew you'd missed the concert I primed the lads not to let it out. But I'd reckoned without dear old Mrs Pearce . . .'

I didn't say a word: didn't know what to say. But I looked at him through a crack of eye. Now he was staring straight ahead with another cigarette on, like a man in a barber's chair waiting for the next bit to happen. So how much did he care – *could* he care, doing what he'd done to us? What real difference did it make to him, us being alive or dead or living in Borneo, apart from whether he had to send the monthly cheque or not? Primed the lads not to let it out! What sort of an idiot did he think I was, that he could try to sit on something like that? Didn't he reckon I might have worked it out for myself – because all the clues had been there, hadn't they? Him loading the drummer's gear, the speed he'd got out of his stage suit, the shirts and bow-ties the others in the band were wearing. I must have been really thick not to have seen it straightaway.

'You must think I'm a right shit.'

I came off the window and looked at him: felt the muscles round my nose pulling. What sort of an expression did you put on your face when you answered 'yes' to a question like that from your dad? Fierce? Or couldn't-care-less? I went back to the window again without deciding, took a great interest in an old Daimler overtaking us.

'I never should've gone off like that. There's no excusing that, Kev.' He flattened his cigarette in the ashtray and lit another one: it must have been his fifteenth that morning. 'Don't expect you to understand that.' There was a great long pause while he dragged in deeply and blew out a thick stream of brown smoke. 'But if I was to tell you, I was bloody close to something else, Kev; something worse; *bloody* close, Kev . . . you might see it a bit different . . .'

I looked him full in the face. You couldn't really pretend to be interested in an old car outside when things like that were being said in the next seat.

'See – what you've got to see – is, before I went I'd had it all ways, Kev. I'd had the security, the army bit, the regular money and the thinking done for me; and I'd had the band – the spotlight, if you like – doing the solos, going all over, getting the applause. And it's a funny thing, what that does to you. It makes you different, doing the solos.' He wasn't looking at me; but I reckoned he didn't need to. He was saying all this for himself. 'See, you're part of the others there with you, and then all at once, you're not, you're on your own. You're taking your solo, and you're chancing your arm. You're nervous; Christ you're nervous all right! But there's no hiding, not then; there's no taking the safe and easy note when *you* know, and you know *they* know, what you've really got to do. In a minute, before you sit down, you're going for the big one, the chancy one, you're going to throw your head back and take that big jump off . . .'

His eyes were closed, and along his cigarette I fancied his fingers were moving ever so slightly in the pattern of some trumpet leap.

'. . . And what people don't know is, that takes a certain sort of *chemistry*, Kev, doing that.' He was back with me, looking me in the eyes. 'Your body, your blood, it adapts to it. See it's like a drug, and it's not up here – ' he tapped his forehead – 'it's physical, in here.' His hand shot down to his stomach. 'And you can't just *stop*. You can't just not do it any more. You're hooked. Your body won't let you just give it up. You can think all the sensible things – Max, you, the responsibility – but, see, that's in your head: while your body's after that drug. And it comes to the push in the end when you either have to have it, or . . . ' He stubbed his cigarette out, not even half smoked, and fished for another one. 'I'll tell you, Kev – ' his voice went all low, and he seemed to be steadying his hand on the seat in front – 'I was *suicidal*. Really. And that's a terrible thing for a man to say when I'd got what I'd got. I used to wander round Thames Reach and wonder how I'd do it . . .' He took in a long, deep breath. 'And then like some miracle along came Freddie Flower. His lead trumpet had had a better offer, Freddie had auditioned one or two, but he wasn't over the moon; and that week I just happened to sit-in at the Empress.' His eyes were burning me; he was desperate that I understood. 'And the chemistry made me go. Nothing else. I just had to . . .'

The coach tyres made that swashing noise as the driver held us steady at about sixty on the flat road. Across the gangway you could see the creases starting to creep into a couple of suits: people's eyes were beginning to close: my chin had just about got over its shave: we were into that long haul that has to happen between the starts and the stops, the main part of the journey which you usually forget.

Usually. But not today. I sat there wondering if such a crucial story had ever been told in the middle lane, going south.

I knew how he'd felt, all right, I'd known it for a long time, or I'd never have let myself even think about the man after he'd gone. I knew because of him, and I knew because of myself. In my own amateur way I was like that with my Hohner, wasn't I? Because it was *all* solo, the Hohner. People made a racket in the fifth-form room while you sucked at your reeds in the corner, then suddenly they were quiet, and all at once you weren't playing for yourself any more, and they knew you weren't, and you didn't dare stop till you'd done it. That was performance. And I knew that chemistry.

So, anyway, why . . . ? What had happened? 'You weren't just the driver, though, not then? Like I used to call you . . . you were the Big Fellow?'

'I was.' He nodded, and heaved a big breath, and got his legs more comfortable. 'This could almost make you laugh, you know. It's just not bloody true! You know why I came out of the Army, don't you?'

'The IRA,' I told him. 'You were going to Ireland – and they even blew up a bandstand in London.' Put a bit blunt like that it suddenly sounded cowardly, but we'd never thought about it that way. 'Max said . . . ' I tried to think how I could make it sound all right.

'I came out to please her, so I wouldn't get blown to bits.' He laughed; and for the first time in my life I knew why they called that sort of thing a hollow laugh. Because it was just that – a laugh forced out of a mouth that wasn't smiling, squeezing out through a little 'O' and echoing because the mouth wasn't wide. And with him smoking, it made a small, swirly smoke ring like the onion he'd dropped off his fork. 'You know what happened, Kev? We were doing this gig in Aldershot – some club in the town, not army – and all of a sudden, while Freddie and me are sharing the mike for 'Chimes Blues', I hear this voice. "Will you stop, please? Will you stop? I've got an urgent announcement." Well, you get that in some clubs when they want to move a punter's car or something, but this guy sounded really serious. So we broke it off, and he quietly tells everyone to get out. No panic, but the police want to search, there's a bomb scare. You should've seen everyone go! Freddie leaves his trombone behind and collars his bottle of Scotch. I follow him off, keeping a tight hold of my silver Boosey, no sweat – but some idiot woman in the front row has only left her handbag on the floor! I jump down, land on it, go over on my ankle, and wallop! flat on the deck – where the bell of my trumpet slices my top lip in half . . .'

Christ! I pulled a face; closed my eyes. I could feel the pain throbbing in my own split lip. In fact, I must have put a hand to it.

'Yeah, just like you. Only a lot worse. I've lost my "lip", Kev. See this scar . . . ?' He spread his mouth like a woman putting on lipstick; and I could see the bump, and just above it the faint white line where the hairs wouldn't grow.

'Oh, I can bash out a tune – of sorts, I've stood in once or twice, but there's none of the old magic any more. I have to play it safe, Kev. There's no more chance of me putting my head back and going for a big one than fly in the air these days.' He ran his trumpet fingers along his mouth. 'To tell you the truth, I'd have got Freddie to let me do something like that last night, if you'd got there in time: it wasn't exactly a big date. See, I can play, Kev, it's just I can't *perform* up to my standard.'

'Don't you reckon I'd have known?' I asked the floor.

He smiled, faintly. 'We'd have fooled you, just the once,' he said, 'rather than . . . ' he suddenly punched his knee. 'What bloody luck, eh? All done! All done – at forty!'

We both went quiet: things running through our heads with the speed of those wheels: but not a lot to say to each other. We were like two cars on the motorway, side by side for a bit, till one of them does some pulling away. He was coming with me for a day or two to sort the licence out, then he'd go back to his driving, and I'd go back to thinking about myself.

I slid a sly look at him. At last he'd caught up with the others in the coach; he'd closed his eyes and let his mouth drop open.

I closed mine. It had all been such a diabolical waste. What poor old Max had been through had been for nothing, in the end. The chance the Big Fellow had taken had turned to crap. Both their lives had been left in messes – with nothing to show for it.

But what about mine? Did I really have to be part of their cock-up, too? Was 'High Pavement Blues' going to be the only tune I could ever tap my foot to? I tried to picture Wendy's face, because at least thinking about Wendy was a little bit hopeful right then. In spite of how ashamed I'd felt that night about Max, I had had a small success there, hadn't I?

Believe it or not, though, her face just wouldn't come. Gone as in goodbye! I could hear her voice all right, saying 'Kev' the way she did, and I could actually feel where we'd been pressed all close together. But instead of her face, whether I closed my eyes or opened them, all I could see was the Big Fellow.

Not surprising. What he'd told me wasn't easy to dump on one side. And I *had* understood what he'd been saying. I'd known the feeling of taking a chance and the kick you get when the chance comes off. And right now, being forced to think about it, I knew what it must be like for someone like that to lose his lip, to be 'all done'. These days, for him, playing something had to be like that terrible time I'd got up on the stall and started shouting the odds all over the High Pavement – when I'd taken the chance, seen for a second or so what it was all about, and then died the death.

Terrible. I felt shattered for him.

And then, right out of the blue, at somewhere near junction seventeen, the memory of that terrible morning – and something he'd said, that 'all done', suddenly rang a bell and I started making a mad grab at an answer. I hadn't been looking for one: but simply because I couldn't shake the tragedy of it from my head, a way out of his terrible situation came rushing at me. 'All done'! the market talk. 'You all done?' It opened my eyes. It sat me up in my seat, just the possibility of it.

Followed straight on by the doubts, of course. How would it sound if I put it to him? And how would he take it? Would it get answered by his mind or by his body? Or had that chemistry thing he'd been talking about gone for good with his 'lip'?

Well, there was only one way to find out. Try him. No harm in that, was there?

All excited, all full of it, I shook him awake. He looked at me with those wild where-am-I? eyes you get when you're suddenly caught out.

'Listen – how about . . . what if . . . hell, the stall!' I said. 'Why don't you come in on the stall?'

He frowned at me; he was still half asleep. 'What stall? What're you on about?'

'Our stall, leather goods,' I said, my hands working over-time like Charlie Cox selling something. 'Why don't you stay down south and work it? Give Max a hand, build it up a bit, go after a few new markets, and, you know, *work* it. Get up on the box and shout the odds.' I was twisted round on the edge of the seat with the pure genius of my idea. '*I've* done it,' I said. 'For a minute, before I sort of fell off; and I can tell you, it's got just what you want; the, you know, the *chemistry*.' The words were falling out. I'd forgotten I was as tired as hell. 'OK, it's not gonna be the same as in some dark theatre, but it's a crowd, a *sort* of audience. They don't come to buy stuff, most of 'em. They come to watch, and listen. It's better than the telly. It's live, and they can have a laugh, hear the smart remarks, see a bit of clever selling . . .'

He was wide awake now, groping for another cigarette in a packet down between us, frowning. 'And you reckon I'd be good at that?'

I gave him a straight look. "Course. You're the sort, aren't you: I am. I reckon I am; I could get good at it – and I'm *your* son.'

'What about Max?' he growled.

I thought for a second. I hadn't forgotten Max, not by a long chalk. 'We'll have to see about Max. 'Course she could put the kibosh on it. But you never know, do you? No one knows for sure what anyone really thinks all the time. No one knows if the bell's got a clapper till they pull the rope.'

He coughed out his cigarette. The first real laugh I'd heard him do. 'God, that's a terrible saying,' he said. 'Where'd you get that?'

'I just made it up.'

'Well, just promise me if I do it you'll let me write my own scripts, eh?'

I punched his arm with pleasure.

'I said, "*If* I do it," ' he muttered, to keep me down.

'Right, "if",' I said back. 'I know. But it's the best thing going till you learn the skins. And it's got to have the edge on driving Freddie Flower's gear in the van. At least it's something you can *tell* people about . . . '

He pulled a face. Stubbed one cigarette out and lit another. And after a bit he started nodding – the way people do when they're getting going on a new idea.

'I swore about it last night; but, who knows, it might have been for the best you *were* late,' he said. 'Else I'd still have been your "Big Fellow" and none of this would've come up . . . '

I shoulder-barged him, there in the seat, and I rabbited on about plans, still going on about how it could work as we pulled off into the services, the one I'd been stopped at, going up: but I didn't give a toss today. We were on the south side now, heading home. And sitting there right next to me was what I reckoned was the answer to all our problems.

The stupidest thing to try and work out in advance was what Max was going to say when I walked in through the flat door dragging the Big Fellow behind me. On the one hand we might get everything melting into one of those misty touches they try on films, with everyone crying on everyone else's shoulder, the violins scraping away, and all of us living happily ever after. On the other, we might get hot soup and the plates and a load of abuse flying through the air. There was no way anyone could tell. So all I could do was make sure we'd done what we could to help things along when we got there.

Today's driver – thank God not Hovis – gave us the standard twenty minutes in the services, and I saw to it that we used every one of them. I needed the Big Fellow looking his best; and I told him, straight. Well, there was no sense pussying about, not with what we'd got depending on it.

'Look at your teeth, Bill; look in the mirror, they're all brown, like your fingers. And I'll tell you, you don't half stink of cigarettes. Don't mind me saying, do you?' If he did, he didn't show it. Perhaps I was going at him too hard for that. 'Tell you what, they might have some of that tooth powder stuff in the shop here – and some scissors; you can cut your nose hairs a bit, you always used to, and your ears; it's growing like a bush out of your ears; and the top of your cheeks . . . '

'Cheers!' he said. But he was nodding, with one of those what-you-have-to-put-up-with-from-your-kids looks. And I was off to the shop already, with a couple of quid he gave me.

They didn't have tooth powder, but they did have Ajax scourer, and a cheap pair of scissors; and before you could say 'Jack Robinson' the Big Fellow was going to it with the corner of his hankie at one of the basins.

As we got back on to the coach I gave him a tube of extra-strong mints I'd bought. 'Have a go at these instead of your fags. And y'can get a shampoo and haircut in London.'

'Good God!' He had to laugh this time. 'Worse than being married, this is!'

'Yeah? You'd better believe it!' I told him. 'There's a lot worse than that, I can tell you!'

It was half past four on that Thursday when we turned the corner of our street. And we'd got it all done. The Big Fellow was a different man, looked like a million dollars; shiny hair, white teeth, smelling like a chemist's. While I felt a hundred years old, all scruffy with my big boots and the Seaford gear, and still looking out from behind that bad lip.

As we went round into view of the house, suddenly I didn't know where my stomach had fallen to. But I definitely knew where my heart was, thumping away nineteen to the dozen: and my head felt as tight as if someone had got me by the throat.

'Come on!' I said, pulling him with me – I wasn't letting either of us stop to think about it now – and we marched up the stairs to the dark, flat door in step.

I had a key on my belt, but I rang the bell. I reckoned you didn't just walk in on someone with a long-lost husband. There was music coming through the letter box, and I thought I heard a bit of singing. But it could have been the blood throbbing inside my head. I did hear the Big Fellow say, 'Going up!' in a quiet voice – as if a show was about to begin.

And then Max opened the door: slim jeans, new hair, tight tee-shirt, and the tilt on her head people have when they've been caught in the middle of a whistle. And she was smiling. A different person, she looked: that puffy-faced drinker with the no-hope eyes had gone, and here was the old Max I'd almost forgotten existed these last few weeks: the one I'd been away to get back, if you like. And there in the doorway I suddenly saw it. It was written all over her. She'd been getting ready for this moment the way the Big Fellow had; just as if she'd known he was coming, as if she'd guessed about my secret trip and had made sure she was looking her best for him. Slowly, so glad about things now, I put my bag inside the door and I smiled at her.

She looked at me, and she looked at him.

'What the hell does *he* want, then? Get washed up on your beach, did he?' She was pushing the door closed already, her face gone all sharp with her change of mood.

'It's the Big Fell . . . it's Dad,' I said.

'I bloody know who it is!'

'Max . . .'

'Don't you "Max" me!' Her face was twisted with dislike.

Now my big boot came in handy, to put into the door. 'Oh, come on, Max,' I said. 'Give him a chance.'

'Give him a chance? *Give him a chance?*' She shouted it at the top of her anger, shooting up on her toes, her neck stretching and her back as brittle and twisted as a used match.

But I got the door open a bit further. God, the terrible feeling of trying to push your way in through your own front door, ever so carefully so you didn't snap your mother with a rough touch.

Gently, very softly, I put an arm round her, I looked into her red, fighting face. 'All I mean is, Max,' I said, 'is listen to him. Just listen to him, then he'll go, if you want him to . . .'

'What the . . . ? Do you mean to . . . ? Have you *fixed this up?*' She looked at me as if I was Charlie Cox. 'Are you telling me this isn't just . . . *accident*, you coming in together?'

'Oh, come on, Max; it's only for a chat. Business . . .'

'*Business?* I've got no business with him!'

But that little bit of talk was just about enough to get us along the narrow passage – the Big Fellow shrugging as if it was all against his will, Max shrinking back against the wall in case the slightest flap of his clothes touched her. I went on ahead into the living room – and my new low spirits took another dive when I saw there wasn't even a seat to sit on. Every flat surface was stacked with stock, piles and piles of it, in boxes and loose: finished bags, half-finished bits, and loads of cheap ready-made stuff bought in new. I couldn't believe it. There was no chance of getting them both relaxed if I couldn't even get them sitting down.

I stood by the kitchen door, the Big Fellow walked over to the window – didn't even put his grip down. And Max stayed out in the passage with her arms folded.

'Listen,' I said, nervous as hell, 'all right, this is down to me. This is Kevin's brilliant idea. And I'm sorry. It's obviously all a big mistake . . . '

Max snorted: a shrieked sort of snort.

' . . . But it's supposed to be just business, right? That's all. Business. A try, to sort out this licence mess. That's all I'm after. Then – '

'What licence mess?' Max still kept back in the doorway, no way ready to come into the same room as the Big Fellow. 'Who said there's a licence mess?'

He put his grip down softly, like one of those reps in a shop, and he held his hands palms out. 'Listen Max, all I've done is come back with the boy to put my name on that piece of paper for you. There's no hassle. Honest. You know me. I'll sign what you want signed, and go. All right?'

That sounded fair enough, I thought. But Max wasn't having any. 'What piece of paper?' she asked.

'The licence. For the stall. Isn't that what you need? It's the least I owe you, love, after what I done . . . '

Now she did come into the room. And with her eyes blazing she stood like some defiant rebel in front of her barricade of stock. 'You don't owe me anything any more, Bill Kendall; you don't owe me anything that isn't strictly legal. And I don't need your signature on *any* piece of paper, thank you very much.'

The Big Fellow dropped his hands and gave me this big, blaming look. *What crap have you been feeding me?* he was asking. I couldn't look at him. I turned away and stared at nothing on the wall. What the hell was Max bluffing about? Why couldn't she put her hands up to things being the way they were? Why not let him do what he wanted to, instead of cutting off her nose this way? It was just stupid pride. Christ, stuff pride! I knew about pride. Hadn't it nearly stopped me getting to know Wendy?

We had to find a way out; just had to. But what came next was this great long silence – the cold sort that gets between people, like a giant ice cube there in the room – and it was obvious Max wasn't going to be the one to try and break it. There was no way she was going to offer even a grunt towards making-up. And I could see that the Big Fellow's mind had gone back to his grip; on to grabbing it and going – as fast as he could get out of the place.

I let it go on as long as I dared. I looked from one to the other of them, standing there staring at one another like two big kids, too grown up to fight and not ready to kiss and make friends. I waited till I saw Max start to back out, for the Big Fellow to actually reach for the handle of his grip; and suddenly I shouted. I hurt my throat to make myself heard in the terrible roar of that silence.

'Listen, you two!' I yelled at them. 'My best, that's all I've done!' I thumped my chest. 'And not for me, you know! No, *you're* the ones in the mess, and all I've tried to do is sort it out. So don't you get the sulks over me!' I swung round on the Big Fellow. '*You* do what *you* want!' I shouted at him; 'and *you* do what *you* want!' I shouted at Max. 'But don't you ever forget it's *me* who's up at six o'clock every Saturday, it's *me* who takes the threats and the abuse and the aggravation off the Coxes, it's me who's had the rough end of all this – and I've had enough of it! OK? So you talk about it like human beings, or you piss off in your different directions. But just don't blame me for trying! Right?' I was crying, nose all running down over my cut lip, hurting myself as I forgot and cuffed it – and suddenly angry for breaking down and making myself hard-done-by. 'Just *talk* to each other at least, for crissake!' I kicked at my Thames Reach bag and crashed off into the kitchen: and stood; and gulped in breath: and had a huge fight with my noisy throat to let me listen.

But there was no need for that. It wasn't five seconds before I was thumped in the back by the door and Max was there, yanking me back into the living room.

'All right!' she gritted. 'All right! I'll talk to you. I'll bloody talk to you both!' She looked all around her, tried to find somewhere to throw me down to listen; but every seat was stacked, and in the end she just twisted me over to the wall with her angry strength and raised her voice instead. 'I'll tell you all about it, *fellows!*' She said it like a new swear word that tasted foul in her mouth.

I got hold of my breathing; and I saw the Big Fellow take his hand off his grip.

'You just went walking out.' She pointed a long, shaking finger at him. 'You went off suddenly one night with your fancy piece, with your little trumpet, and it's all big deal, and doing it for your art, and you're nothing but a . . . *pawn* . . . in the hands of this great talent. The poor helpless artist, following his heart. And everyone says, "Old Bill's gone off – run away with the circus" and "Poor old Max, how's she going to manage, with the boy an' all?" But all the time everyone knows she will, somehow. Because everyone knows she's got to. And she does! And she bloody *does* manage! But if it had been me going off, well, there's a different story. "The wicked little slut, the Jezebel!" But not the jazzer-boy! Oh, no! Max is left to slave her guts out, and no one takes a blind bit of notice! No help. Friends disappear. And never mind what *she* might have wanted out of life. "She's got her leather, hasn't she?" Well, too right, she has. And a bloody good job, too, because what used to be a hobby has got to be her life-line. Sink or swim, that's what it's been for me!'

She took in a big breath, too quick to allow an interruption. 'And Kevin plays his part. Fair's fair. Kevin plays his part. But it is only a part. It's my life!' She made us jump by suddenly screaming it. 'It's my bloody *life!*'

There was no moving your eyes, or a foot. Even your breathing had to be done carefully.

'And I've made a go of it – because I've had to. A good go, till suddenly things go wrong. Suddenly, the council puts its oar in, there's a spot of bother, and what is it?' She stopped, waited for an answer which no one gave, and twisted round to look at me: stood and waved these two shaking arms in my face and shouted in a high kid's voice, ' "Get Daddy. Tell a pack of lies and get the Big Fellow to come and sort it out"!' She spun round back on him. 'And, "Oh what a gem!" you can hear them saying, "See? He'd never leave you in the lurch when it really comes to it"'!'

She stopped, stood trembling, her face red, heaving in breath in great gulps. It was uncomfortable as hell. I shifted my feet a bit: but I wanted to shift my whole body – something like a couple of miles away, because I could have taken the truth, but that wasn't the way it was, not my part in it. My mind hadn't worked like that at all. It was fright had made me go: fright at her drinking, fright at the Coxes, fright at what I'd done by going off to Wendy's. But what was the use? How did you start to tell them that?

I didn't get a chance to anyway, because Max had started on again.

'But, relax! It's all sorted out, chaps. It's done! See? The problems over, and here's the proof, all round you.' She waved her arm at the stock on the settee and chairs. 'So you're not required, Bill Kendall, you can go back where you came from – and you can make your mind up, Kevin, just what *you* want to do!'

She was really close to tears; but holding herself in by putting her hands on her hips and staring hard at me.

Make my mind up? What she was saying was, was I going to stay with her, or clear off with the Big Fellow? Shit, I'd never seen it coming to that. Why the hell did everything have to be so black and white, so either or? Why couldn't everyone muddle along in the grey for a bit?

Now the Big Fellow did pick up his grip. 'Fair enough, Max,' he said. 'I won't argue with none of that. Can't. Except over Kevin. Just be fair on Kevin, eh? He's only done what he thought was for the best, believe me. But as for Bad Bill Kendall, right, I put my hands up. Did just what you said. Only don't blame me for what other people say. Don't blame me because I wasn't slapped all over the *News of the World*. That's other people's business, what they say. Ours is ours . . .' He stopped by the door, seemed to be trying to find one or two more words. But he couldn't, and he started to go.

Suddenly, I was over on that side of the room, getting hold of his grip. 'Hold on!' I yelled. 'If I could just have three minutes more of you two together.' I turned to Max, took a deep breath, dropped my voice, tried to sound about as hostile as a rabbit. 'So how did you do it Max? Last I knew they were kicking us out . . .'

Max gave me one of those looks that'll never blink. 'I thought you might want to know,' she said. She pushed past the Big Fellow into the passage and came back with a plastic-wrapped leather briefcase. 'I did it with this, believe it or not – and no thanks to you, Kevin!'

It was the briefcase the Coxes had used to rub my nose in it that day, after they'd shut me up from shouting the odds: the one the policeman had taken a shine to when he'd come to see about the watches. That briefcase, or one just like it.

'Remember this? The day you got clever? Being offered at a give-away price? Well, I've not been in the business this long for nothing, I'll tell you. Cheap watches, all right, but there was no way he was shifting these at silly prices without them being bent. So I looked into it: got someone to buy me one, gave it a good going-over: and see what I found, burnt out with an iron and polished over?' She lifted the flap of the briefcase and showed me, just above the catch where it wouldn't notice closed: a sort of scar where a maker's name had been, just above the tooling REAL LEATHER.

'See, they saw to this, but they forgot about the catch. You can always tell a good case by its brasswork.' Like a woman with the whitest washing on the telly, she showed me the catch-maker's name. 'One or two phone calls was all it took and I'd got who they'd made the catches for. A few more, and I knew who'd lost them off the back of a lorry . . .'

My mouth must have dropped open because it felt very dry all of a sudden. So she'd done with the cases what I'd tried to do with the watches. And she'd pulled it off where I hadn't.

'So now you know why I was so bloody angry with you for trying that trick with the police. I was just at the beginning of all this!'

'You could've said, then – instead of slinging soup. Could've saved me a bit of bother, too, you know . . .'

'It was early days, Kevin.' She rattled on, talking fast. 'I didn't know what I was going to do for sure. And I was depressed that first week, up one day, down the next. But you helped make my mind up – because instead of going to the police, guess where I went after you'd gone to Seaford?' She didn't give time for an answer. 'To Cox, that's where I went. To his Monday market over Stratford. And with what I'd got here, and the papers to say who'd bought it and where from, we came to a business agreement, Charlie Cox and me . . . '

'God alive! Did you?'

'Too right, I did. He's not bidding for my pitch, and he's making sure no one else does, either: and I'm keeping my trap shut about his briefcases.' She stood there all proud, staring at the Big Fellow. Then she turned her eyes back on me. 'Wasn't easy, mind. Nothing is, with them. And I needed Alfie on my side – but he could see I meant business.'

I forced out a smile: pleased for her, but choked that it had all got sorted out without my plan for the Big Fellow coming into it. And that hurt a lot more than a split lip ought to make it.

But the Big Fellow was still in the room, and now he said something, as if he had to remind us of the fact. He put his grip down, and sat on it.

'This Alfie: Kevin said about him. How d'you get round a hard little case like that?'

Max looked at the Big Fellow, very suspicious. Why this great interest all of a sudden? she was asking. All the same, there was no way she could sit on that part of the story.

'*You* know Alfie's little game, don't you, Kevin? You've seen it.'

'Which one?' He had a million.

'I threatened Alfie I'd tell his old man about his cash fiddle if he didn't go along with what I wanted.'

I looked at the floor, stared at the carpet all littered with pieces of packing paper. That one! Yes, I knew about Alfie's cash fiddle all right, just how he did it, but I'd never had the guts to say anything about it in case I was forced to face Charlie with it; I'd been bottling out of that for the best part of two years. Now it turned out Max had known as well, and she'd known I knew and I hadn't dared to say. All at once I didn't feel quite so sure of myself over what I'd done in all this. Who knows, with a bit more red blood in me we might've played on Alfie before.

'Tell us, then, what was this Alfie's fiddle?' He was showing a real interest, the Big Fellow. At least it kept the talking going.

Max looked at me, but told the tale herself. 'Alfie? Well, if you really want to know, he's this big kid, works the pitch with his old man, nice looking boy – and rotten as old meat inside. Sometimes gets up and sells, but mostly stays down on the ground passing out the goods and taking the money. Anyway, the way he works it, nine times out of ten he takes the goods off the old man with his left hand to pass them out, and he takes the money off the punter with his right – stuffs it into his right hand pocket. But about every tenth sell – more or less, right, Kevin? – he takes the goods with his right, and he puts the punter's money in his left pocket.' She was explaining it straight to the Big Fellow now, normal voice, the way she used to tell him something late at night after he'd come in from a concert. 'And the only money Alfie ever puts into the pot – they've got this big china thing for the takings, down in front of Charlie – is what comes out of his right hand pocket. The rest is bunce, Alfie's rake-off. And he's been doing that for ages.' She came back to me, eyebrows raised, and I nodded. 'Well, I reckoned his old man would just about kill him if he knew: and I reckon I'm right, the way Alfie gave in when I got him on his own over Stratford . . .'

She'd gone all red in the face again; not because she was angry this time, but because she was proud. Well, you need to share a victory like that. Now she came down to earth and remembered how much she didn't need him.

'So I can do without your autograph on the application form,' she said. 'It's all sewn up, just about. Thank you very much.'

That should have been the end of it: but something made him go for one more try. Instead of picking up his grip and going, he stood where he was and looked round the room at all the cardboard boxes.

'So you've bought in stock,' he said. 'You're not just selling what you make yourself?'

'That's right. For what it's worth to you, I'm done with the Saturday image. I'm going for more. I've got this lot on credit, and I'm getting a loan on a van. And I've booked a course of driving lessons, so I can work some of the other markets . . .'

I slid down the wall and sat on the floor. All in six days! It's amazing what a bit of success can do to someone. After sorting out Charlie Cox she'd gone on and re-organized her whole life.

She'd re-organized my life, too, if you thought about it; except there was no thinking about anything just then, because the Big Fellow had taken another step back into the room and was talking to her in a quiet Adam's apple sort of voice.

'Well, as it happens, Max, I've got to tell you, I really came back with young Kev to do a bit more than just sign that licence – if you'd wanted it . . .'

Max was staring at him as if he was selling her a vacuum cleaner she didn't want.

'No . . . I came down to see if you'd . . . like . . . well, let me come back. Just business, if you like. To kick off with. Purely business . . .'

'Eh?' her voice went through an octave and took five seconds over the incredulous word.

'Strictly in line with the way you're thinking, Max. You know, developing, expanding. Different lines. Getting up and doing a bit of selling – you know, do the business with the crowd . . .'

He dried up: he wasn't so good at selling himself as he'd be with a new line in suitcases. And Max's eyes were out on stalks.

'Are you *joking*?' She looked round as if she was after something to throw at him.

'No, I'm not joking. It's a serious business proposition, Max.'

She leant against the back of a chair.

'I can't believe it. Are you saying you're prepared to give up your Jack-the-lad, solo trumpet life for standing up on a bloody market stall . . . ?'

'Max . . .' He dodged the answer, put out a hand.

'No, come on, let's get this straight. Are you telling me you care so much about me that you'll do that? *So* much, that you'll say *that* to your trumpet?' She snapped her fingers, loud and successful.

And now the Big Fellow looked back at me. Because I knew, and he knew, that he wasn't really going to be giving up anything. The solo-in-the-spotlight, Jack-the-lad life wasn't his any more to give up.

From where I was on the floor I looked at him, and I looked at her; and I tightened my grip round my knees.

But he didn't say a word, and neither did she: while the whole room, with the three of us and all that stock in it waited for what was going to be said next. Nothing. Another great silence: but not the ice cube sort this time: more the vacuum. And I knew that a hell of a lot depended on who broke it. Because if he did the talking, and said he was giving up his silver trumpet to come back and throw in with her, I had a funny feeling there was just an outside chance she'd say 'yes'. But if I did the talking, and I came clean about what I knew – then he'd probably find his way to the street via that window he was standing by.

And he wasn't saying anything. He wasn't saying 'yes' to her question, and he wasn't saying 'no'. He was definitely leaving the decision about what Max was told to me, the man in the middle.

I couldn't grip those legs any tighter. I could feel my feet going to sleep where they were being starved of blood.

So, it was down to me, then, to give this family a chance to get back together. And a quiet nod, that's all it wanted, I knew that. Just let the Big Fellow know I'd keep my mouth shut while he played himself in.

Or I could go for nothing but the whole truth now, no matter what.

Max cut into the silence. 'I said, so you're ready to give all that up, are you? All that *stardom*, to come back to me?' Her fists were balled up tight, the strings standing out on her arms. She'd got to know – before she either kicked him out or let him stay.

The Big Fellow looked at her and sort of smiled. 'Max . . .' he said, right down in his throat, 'it never sounds enough just to say it, but . . . I'm sorry, Max . . . ' He put his hand out, and let it drop.

But he wasn't really saying it: not what he had to, the honest truth about where he stood. He could well have been sorry; I didn't doubt that for a minute. But was he building up trouble for himself by not saying *everything*?

And that still left me with the worst decision I'd ever had to make in my life. Let it out, or let it go. Agree with him keeping quiet, with all that could mean if Max found out; or risk making sure they never came back together.

I hated it. I resented it. I felt bitter inside. I even tasted it in my mouth, because it wasn't fair, landing that on me. I hurt my arms, hugging. Life wasn't fair, people weren't – right down to that bloody coach driver! If I hadn't been late in Steelton I'd never have known the truth about the Big Fellow: I'd still have seen him as one of Freddie Flower's All Stars. And while there wouldn't have been a chance he'd come back, there wouldn't have been this diabolical decison for me to make, either.

But something must have been going on all that time inside my brain, making up my mind for me, because at that moment I surprised myself by slowly standing up, pushing my back up the wall and stamping my boots like a guardsman where the pins and needles hurt. And without even knowing I was thinking about it, a second before they did, I found out I wasn't going to bottle out of this crisis after all. You could say I'd done enough of that!

The Big Fellow was looking to me for the word. And now I knew what that word was going to be. Tough, but true. There was no way the Kendalls could go on as a family without everybody's cards face up on the table, no cheating, that's the way I felt. It was John Wayne stuff: but where it was needed, for once.

'Aldershot, Dad,' I said. 'Weren't you going to tell Max about Aldershot . . . '

He looked at me, and closed his eyes, and took in this great, deep breath.

'You're right, Kev,' he said. 'Yeah. There is something I was meaning to tell you, Max . . . '

And while we all stood there in that hell room like a family round a grave, he started to tell the truth about himself to her tense, white face.

Chapter Ten

I got out and kicked around Thames Reach, my head filled with all the names they were throwing at one another: insulting things which showed how far apart they were. Things like 'smug', 'smart-arse', 'bra-burner' – they were for her – and 'selfish', 'traitor', 'failure' – they were for him. Even 'gigolo'. *Gigolo!* That sad old man! It stuck in my mind the most, kept coming back in a chant as if the *Kop* was jumping up and down to it: 'Gigolo, gigolo, gigolo . . . ' What was going on back there was all so different to the way I'd pictured them coming together in my head, those nights a long time ago when I'd cried myself to sleep. And not a bit like the way I'd seen it on the coach, either, when my business proposition seemed to give us a ray of hope. It was too depressing for words.

They didn't even see me go as I pushed past them out of that tip of a living room, them swearing at one another, and me swearing at myself for being so George Washington honest. Straight off I could see I'd made a big mistake – because who in the world can really take the plain unvarnished truth? Which two people don't depend on a bit of what-the-eye-doesn't-see to keep them going? God alive, we all do our fair share of acting – why the devil couldn't I have let the Big Fellow do his?

It was getting quite dark, and cold again. My lip hurt a lot, and so did my lumped-up throat: but I was much better off out than in. I covered a lot of ground. I walked along past Smith's, down by the dockyard near Nick's house and through the little twist of back streets which led towards the Albion Club. Everywhere was quiet, not even the sound of television coming through the windows: and with no one to be seen in all that build-up of houses and flats, I felt like the only person in the world that night. Even the football ground, where all that aggravation went on, seemed to be asleep. It was lonely as death.

I walked, and I swore at myself, and I went into all the *ifs* of the last few days till my head went round and round. But my body, just as it had that night with Wendy, somehow seemed to steer my feet without me thinking about it – took me through the Albion Estate, up to the parade ground, and then over the Wellcome roundabout to the ring road; and within twenty minutes or so I found myself where I might have known I was going all the time. On to Wendy's doorstep, chiming at her bell, and doing a stupid, nervous dance, because I was going to see her.

Mrs Goodchild opened the door.

'Oh, it's Kevin!' She sounded really pleased to see me. 'Come in, come in. Wendy, it's Kevin! Lord, what have you done to your mouth?'

'Oh, I had a bit of an accident.'

'I should say you did. Hurry up, Wendy, Kevin's here.'

It's a crazy thing, but I still couldn't picture Wendy's face till she came to that door. But when I did, and I saw her smile, I knew just why I'd had to get out of our place in a hurry and come here. There was this warm, sweet feeling that seemed to just trickle inside like biting a liqueur chocolate: something very special that doesn't happen every day of your life.

All I could hope was that she wasn't put off me by my ugly lip.

Mrs Goodchild had gone. Wendy didn't say a thing: she looked at me, frowned, and suddenly kissed me, there on the bad place.

'Who's had a war with you?' she asked.

'Me. Did it to myself, the other night.'

She just stared. I could see her going over the what and the how. Then, 'You silly idiot!' she said, took my hand and led me into the sitting room.

I let myself be taken, just stood next to her in the calm and stillness. That was what I liked about that room: that's what I'd remembered: the peace. If there'd been any dust about you'd have heard it falling into the carpet. In the alcove there was more blue glass, on the bookshelf were the Sinatra tapes, and over by the unplugged telly, Wendy's dad's moccasins nestled under a radiator. It was a leisure room, a place where no work was meant to go on – a whole life-style away from the stacks of stock and the smell of glue back in Rope Street.

We didn't say a thing, not for ages. We held hands; we found the settee; we remembered how we snuggled on it; and with Mrs Goodchild's sewing machine on the go in the background, Wendy gently started to heal my lip and give me back a bit of hope.

My memory hadn't played a single trick on me. Being here with Wendy again was everything I'd wanted it to be: all warm and soft and loving, making me feel a hundred times better, like a sort of miracle medicine.

Quietly and slowly, looking up at the fancy pink ceiling, I started to tell her what had happened: how I'd decided to try to find the Big Fellow; and then how my beat-up face and the Thames Reach bag had got me taken off the coach to Steelton. It took a long time to tell because she would sympathize, and keep on sympathizing, and I've never felt so spoilt in all my life. I lay back there lapping it up. And then I got on to the rest: about what missing the concert had meant; how I'd brought the Big Fellow back; and the last part of the story, the ructions at home, and the terrible words that had chanted in my head as I walked away out of it. Wendy started to laugh at *gigolo*; but suddenly she stopped, went stiff, and gripped tight on the muscle of my arm. 'I reckon I'd die,' she said, 'if that ever happened to me . . .'

The way she said it almost made me want to cry: suddenly I felt sorry for myself again, the way I had when he first went, because it *had* happened to me, all this. But I held it back: God, imagine lying there crying! I tried hard to concentrate on the nice, calm things she was saying, on her telling me how she'd been thinking about me, and what she'd been doing in the past six days: but, to be honest, I really wasn't listening. I was thinking about what she'd said at first. *I'd die if that ever happened here*. And as I thought about it I reckoned I knew why: she'd die because it *couldn't* happen here: it just couldn't, you could tell from the three of them.

And I thought about the Big Fellow, who'd made it happen to us, thought about the sort of person he was, and how he couldn't fit in here if you paid him – and I started to wonder.

Hadn't I had it all wrong? I'd gone along for years with one idea in my head about what success was; and that was the Big

Fellow's sort of success, the solo spot, the acclaim. But wasn't this, right here, as much a success as a round of applause? Didn't all this show what you could do with your life just as much as hitting a tricky note at the end of a solo did? Did you really have to have a thousand people cheering you to get the feeling you'd made it? You couldn't help thinking Wendy's mum and dad with their happy home had got as much to feel proud of as the Big Fellow and Freddie Flower had when they blew the blues.

Which, as I lay there thinking about it, all came down to me asking what sort of a life I really fancied for myself. Did I still want to be like the Big Fellow in some way, as I always thought – the solo person who gets up and does his thing, regardless? Or would I settle for being like Wendy's dad, with what he'd helped to get going here?

God! What a question for a Thursday night! And I didn't find out the answer. There was this dig in my ribs all of a sudden – it's weird how some people are born able to hit the spot – and Wendy was being all offended. 'Casanova's miles away!' she moaned.

I pulled myself up and we talked a lot more. We drank tea, she stroked my neck when we said goodnight on the doorstep, and I walked home feeling tons better than I had when I'd come. But, I knew, not half as good as I would when I found out the answer to the big new question I'd started asking myself.

Whatever was stewing inside me, Max had a fantastic Friday. I couldn't remember when I'd seen her so full of herself. It was a bit as if she'd just been told she wasn't going to die of something after all, and suddenly everything she saw or touched seemed to be big deal to her. I saw her peeling off a cup-cake with a smile on her face as if the secret of the universe was inside; and actually laughing at a man on the telly she usually threw things at.

Of course, you didn't need to be a genius to know why. The pitch was hers, and she'd got a peace treaty of sorts with the Coxes, but that wasn't all of it: that much had got her on to her feet while we were still pounding down the M1: no, what had lifted her off the floor and sent her dancing round the flat was feeling square with the Big Fellow. She'd shown him she could look after herself, that there'd been no reason for him to come speeding home as if he was some knight in armour, that he could be done without. He'd gone off to a life without her: now she'd shown she was quite happy living her life without him. It was as simple as that.

And when she drank her Bacardi and Coke after I got in from Wendy's it was for the taste, and not for what it did to her. Which was all very nice for Max: and, OK, I'd been worried sick enough about her to have tried all sorts of tricks for a change like this. But all the same, I couldn't feel good about it. She was acting like one of a couple of kids you might see in the school yard. *He did it to me so I've got to do it back to him!*

It wasn't the world's biggest surprise to see the Big Fellow had gone when I got back from Wendy's. It was as if he'd never been. All the words seemed to have blown out of the window, and the place was filled with the business. The new stock, rustling with tissue, was all stacked and tidied; there were seats to sit on again; and in her work-room Max had started on a fancy waistcoat in midnight blue.

'New season's colour,' she told me in a voice like the old days. 'We'll have a whole rack of these, exclusive. Out before Christmas up West, so they'll be all the go in Thames Reach by Easter!'

Not a word about him. It was as if he'd vanished off the face of the earth: and with her so happy I didn't feel like asking. She went on as if nothing had happened, so I played her game and watched her for a while.

She was a great worker; a real artist herself; she handled that leather in a way that somehow seemed to make it help her, as if she and the material were both singing the same song. And you could see the waistcoat she was making would be really special – there wouldn't be another one quite the same as that in the world. As exclusive as Paris, was what Max made.

Putting my disappointment over the Big Fellow on one side, it made me good to see that talent on show again. It gave me a bit of hope – for her and for me, at least. It made me think what a waste it'd be if the Coxes and the council had won and she just stopped doing it. Talents like that *need* to be used. Almost without realizing it I found myself finding words to describe what she was making: *soft as moonlight on your shoulder* – that was a good one, I was pleased with that: *a beautiful blue, in leather for ever*: not so hot, but going in the right direction. At least I got a kick out of doing that for a few minutes. I put a whole string of things together in my head, a line of patter someone could stand up and shout at a crowd: the Big Fellow for preference, of course; but even me if it came to it. Something a little bit *creative*: enough to say without drying up: something I was pleased with.

But when the words in my head had run out, I left Max to it and wandered into the living room. I sat on the settee, hard, to try to make the cushion body-shaped again instead of moulding to the marks of the boxes. I knew a bit about settees now, I reckoned; and I'd never forget this one as long as I lived. This settee was Max, drunk out of her mind, and Max, the new stock. And that was all, sad to say.

I laid-in late, that Friday: thinking, mostly. And when I got up I walked round and round the place going over what was worrying me. I didn't say a lot: went in now and then and told Max I liked her new stuff, did some staining for her, sorted some of the new stock and priced-up the tickets – and even tried to do some geography. But the real life was going on inside my head: over and over, that bugging and buzzing about me. It might seem stupid, but somehow I *needed* to know – what sort of a person was I? What was I made of? It would have helped a lot to have got out the Hohner and talked into that: that might have told me something, who knew? But thanks to my own idiot fist I still couldn't touch it, so I had to do without the shutting my eyes and making new sounds to see how I felt. Then again, perhaps it was the sort of answer you couldn't force out.

Meanwhile, I lived for the evening. What got me through that churned up day was the thought of Wendy Goodchild, of seeing that smile when she opened the door, hearing her say, 'Hello, Kevin' in that special belonging sort of way. After our meal I rushed through Thames Reach like a cat let out: and for a couple of hours I got away from all my worries. But as I dawdled home in the chilly dark, back they came again like ghosts to haunt me. Kevin Kendall and what he was; the Kendall family and what the future held. For the first half-hour, all the way back to the Wellcome Roundabout and over it, I plagued myself with deep, long term doubts about us all. But as the Royal Artillery loomed and low tide on the river brought Thames Reach into the nostrils, that other worry came worming in to drive out all the others. Tomorrow. Saturday.

My life was notched in Saturdays. I was *scarred* by them. Whatever else I might have to think about, that regular weekly misery swept round like a scythe and still had me jumping.

It was all about Alfie Cox, of course. Alfie Cox, the old enemy for ever: because getting things straight between him and Max didn't matter a toss when it came to me. He'd find a way to pay me out all right, I knew that. Like with kids at school: the headmaster might tell your mother he's sorted out some bit of bother; but that's never the real end of the story. There's always the last sly kick to remind you who's really king of the castle. So, getting all stewed up about myself and the family might have kept the knees from knocking for a bit; but as Saturday loomed they became problems that were much less urgent – rather like worrying where heaven is when you're out desperately looking for Catford Town Hall.

And as sure as the sun, round it came, that Saturday morning. The Big Ben Repeater took another dent as it hit the bedroom floor: and I was back in the old routine. I went through the motions of getting washed and dressed the way you do on exam days, letting the small things help get me through: like making a big decision about which sweater to wear – the man about to be executed asking for a soft-boiled egg.

I looked in the mirror. I must have changed in some ways since last week, mustn't I? Grown? Got older? Those seven days had seen enough other things changing. But, no luck – it was the same old Kevin Kendall looking back, jumpy and grey, just the split lip different: the same kid scared stiff because he'd got to go out in the cold again and set that stall up on his own.

I felt like going in and serving up that fact to Max with her early cup of tea. 'Did you know, Max – I *could* have had another pair of hands with me today?' But I left it – pride, probably; and quite a bit of shock! Because instead of her drab old dressing gown, she was up making her first moves in jeans and a bra: ten years younger.

Well, someone had changed all right!

I drank a glass of milk extra and pulled on my duffel.

'I'm off now.'

'See you later, Kev.'

'Yeah, see you.'

And now the old battle was on again, the one where the rules wouldn't have changed as far as I was concerned. And, as usual, the big question was, could I beat the Coxes to the High Pavement today? I shouted a last goodbye to Max, skidded out of the house, put my head down and ran along Rope Street; got to the road behind the market, jumped over crates of wet salad, did a slippery dance on the cobbles, and raced for the yard where the stalls were kept. In the gateway I stood to catch my breath and forced myself to look. Was Coxes' stall in there? Blast! It had gone. Alfie Cox was out there and waiting.

Mouthing all sorts of filth to myself, I got a grip on the fat handles of our own stall, all wet and splintery, and giving it a heave to get the rusty wheels going, I pulled it out away from the wall. It seemed heavier than ever, as if I'd lost a load of strength in the week, but as the sweat broke out and pricked my back in the cold, I finally got it rolling. Turning round, I bent myself over and ran it out through the gates on to the bone-shaking cobbles in front of the High Pavement. I took the biggest breath I could draw. Now for the big, gut-splitting effort. I put my head down and charged for the steps like a sailor with a gun at the Royal Tournament.

But it was easy. It was so easy it wasn't true: it was as if they'd smoothed those cobbles out, or I'd got my wheels in the tram lines: the thing came rolling along behind me like a really good push in the back. Great stuff! So I *had* changed, after all, to be able to put on sudden strength like that! It wasn't till my running feet lifted clean off the ground that I found out. God alive, I *was* being pushed!

'Go on!' he shouted. 'Go on!'

It was the Big Fellow – smart, young, Jack-the-Lad almost.

I didn't break step: I took four more strides to the High

Pavement, got my feet on it and then stopped, grabbing for breath. 'You . . . ?' I said. 'What the . . . ?'

'Couldn't stand by, watching, could I? I just came up from down the gents and there was this rickshaw boy having a struggle . . . ' He leant on the barrow. He was more exhausted himself than he wanted to let on.

But he was around. He hadn't given up. He was hanging on for a chance. Had to be, because he certainly wasn't driving the band up in Scotland, and look how he was trying.

It was like some ton weight being lifted off my shoulders. It was what I'd prayed for every Saturday morning since God knew when: a bit of family to be with me in my war with Alfie Cox: a bit of support.

And what was good, he'd come to give me a hand, not a row for what I'd forced him into telling Max. Under all those layers I puffed up my chest. Perhaps I *had* been right, then – if he thought he still had a chance. Perhaps now that the poison had been let out they could start to put the ointment on. I took it as a good sign, anyway.

It went up the High Pavement like a dream, the stall. I pulled it along the line like some little kid on Open Day who's showing off his dad to the others: and I twisted it into our space with a big flourish I was annoyed that Alfie missed.

But Charlie was there; and I saw the Big Fellow weighing him up, putting a finger to his scar like he did all the time; but we got on, put the chocks down, lashed up the framework, and Charlie hardly seemed to notice.

I couldn't make my mind up whether I was pleased or sorry our space was clear. In some ways it would've been good for the Big Fellow to see what I had to put up with. On the other, perhaps it meant Max had 'done the business' all right. Perhaps I'd been too pessimistic and our troubles were over.

Pigs might fly! Who was I trying to kid? They might be with Charlie, but the absent Alfie had something up his sleeve for me, I could stake my life on that: something between just him and me: something I couldn't go running to Max about . . .

And I was right. But I had to wait a while to find out what it was. I had to wait till the stall was rigged, the lights plugged in and the Big Fellow had slid away with a smile and a confident,

'See you later, Kev . . . ' Then I saw him. Just an elbow on the sill of their cab at first, then a pair of eyes and a cunning smile.

'Well, if it ain't little Saturday! 'Ad a bit of a 'and, 'ave you, son? Daddy come back from 'is naughties?'

'Shut your mouth!' I said. 'I'm busy.'

"Course you are, Saturday, 'course you are. Ain't we all? But I did just want a little word in your ear, Ugly. Just suthin I wanna get straight with you . . . '

'Well, there's nothing I want to get str? ʒht with you . . . '

He sprang. Suddenly, he had his cab door open and he was half out, leaning up over it like some meaty preacher, pointing his finger down at me as if I'd been up to something disgusting in the churchyard.

'I know what you been doin'. I know your little games, son. *All* about the Old Bill. Well, there's a million ways I can make your life 'ell, Saturday, whether Daddy's 'ere or not. 'He grinned at me, just enjoying being bigger than I was. And suddenly he shook the door at me, made me jump back and crack my spine against our stall. "S'all right, I ain't gonna 'it you,' he sneered. 'Would I 'it a little puke like you, an' 'ave you runnin' to Mummy? No, son, I'm gonna get you in a way you can't tell Mummy about. I'm gonna learn you a few facts o' life. Like with your little Wendy, for a start. 'Cos I fancy a nibble at that myself.' He flashed out a comb from his back pocket and flicked his hair with it. 'You see 'er come runnin' my son, when Alfie calls . . . '

He jumped out of the cab, slammed it shut, and stood staring down at me while his words sank in. And before I could think of a word of my own to say – leave out anything to do – he'd lifted up a corner of our tarpaulin and thrown it over my head.

'That's better, Saturday. I can't bear ugliness no better'n a good looking bird can.' And by the time I'd fisted my way out from under it he was round the front with Charlie, throwing up heavy boxes as if he'd been doing it all morning.

I left the stall, walked back home through the market, stepped round other people's stacks, minded my back from barrows when the little kids call: but all I could think about were the ugly words of Alfie's threat. I told myself he didn't know Wendy like I did: I could be as sure about her as I could be about

149

anything. But nothing in life was a cast iron certainty, was it – and he knew all right where I could be got at these days. The only bit of my life that seemed to be working out at all. I had tons to do to keep up at school, I was in a right state over Max and the Big Fellow, and I couldn't put my Hohner to my lips to save my life. But I'd got Wendy Goodchild and her smile to keep me going, to stop me from turning loony, and now Alfie was out to do for that.

And he was dead right in what he'd said. There was no running to your mother about girl friend troubles. And if I told Charlie about the trick with the takings, what price my legs?

I got home for my breakfast and swallowed a bit of it down somehow. Max drank tea and sang with the radio, didn't seem to notice anything. And I couldn't even find the guts to tell her the Big Fellow had been around.

Together, me with one eye all around, we got the stall set up. There was so much new stock we could hardly get it all on. It even started to look as if *we* could be the ones who needed to hustle for extra space. We made a really good display of as much as we could – there's nothing about a cardboard box to turn a customer on – and with the bought-in lines hanging all round from fresh hooks, and the good gear Max was making stuck in the front, the stall had a life about it which it hadn't had since Max and the Big Fellow first set it up. And she had so much of her old sparkle back that a sort of electricity crackled over the High Pavement like lightning.

All of which was great. A fortnight before I'd have settled for that like a shot, thought it was Christmas. But now I was more upside down than I'd ever been with everything about me so uncertain – and especially Alfie's threat to split up Wendy and me. I tried to tell myself that perhaps that always happens when you get to my age – you start looking at yourself and you get all unsure, you need to keep hold of what you've got *because* you're in a state. But it didn't help. Didn't shift the pain an inch.

We got quite busy mid-morning, both of us serving a lot of the time. Max had been right, some of the new cheaper lines were just what people wanted. But I couldn't keep myself busy enough to stop worrying about what would happen with Alfie when Wendy came round: and I got to the pitch of not even wanting her to. What rotten trick had he got up his sleeve? Because you could bet your bottom dollar he'd pull some stunt.

And he did. He must have been watching for her as hard as me, because as soon as I saw her shining hair and that special smile come dancing along the High Pavement, making her way round the back of the crowd Charlie was working, he suddenly jumped up next to his old man, said something in his ear, banged the box, and took over the selling, just like that. The old man shrugged, shuffled to one side, lit a cigarette as much as to say, 'Get on with it, then,' – and left it to Alfie, King of the Castle. I swore: got a mean look from Max: but there was nothing I could do for the minute except watch. This was the second time he'd done this – and I couldn't shake the horrible thought that on the first time he'd very near done for Wendy and me.

"Ere y'are, ladies and gents, Alfie's the name, sellin's the game, and don't no one move a muscle. One more inch, girl, and believe me, you've lost the chance of a lifetime!'

It was quick and cheeky, anything-might-happen, the sort of thing people like about young comics, and sure enough it worked like magic to stop people pushing past. Up on my toes, I could see Wendy trapped where she was, hemmed-in tight enough to have to listen to him for a minute.

'Now then, girls, knowin' me you won't be surprised if I tell you what I've got to show is a bit special!' He winked, all sexy, and a couple of old ladies cackled. 'Do you wanna see it? Do you? Never mind the old man, who wants to see something special – a real exclusive line?' He looked around like an auctioneer. 'Lovely young lady there – ' he was pointing at Wendy, who else? – ' beautiful girl like you likes nice things, I'll bet, eh?'

Wendy went red and tried to stare him out.

'Be a sport, darlin': be fair an' give me two minutes, 's'all I ask . . .' She couldn't move now, that was for sure.'. . . an' if you tell me you've seen anything like this, I'll give up, I will, honest to God.'

He clapped his hands, four right fingers into his left palm, and out of nowhere he twirled a neat, square cardboard box into the air: started to open it, all spread fingers like a refined tea drinker. 'Now just 'ave a peep at this an' tell me if it ain't one of the most beautiful things you've ever seen . . .'

My eyes darted his way and hers as I strained on my toes to keep track of what he was pulling. Because this was all part of his getting at me, there was no doubt about that.

She'd had to stop trying to get past. He'd got her there for the moment, had her looking at him, squinting in the light. And the rest of them too. A bit of humour and a lot of pull had got the whole crowd watching to see what he was going to show them.

From the box in his hand he took something small wrapped in white tissue, held it up high. 'Hand-made by master crafts-men,' he said. He started unwinding the layers, like a collector with treasure, taking his time till the tissue finally came off.

I stared at what it was. I couldn't believe it! My stomach did another somersault inside. The clever bastard! He knew what he was about, all right. In his hand, held up high in the cool sun, was a boy in deep blue glass, a beautiful thing, classic, letting the light shine through in that peaceful sort of way blue glass does.

'Is that nice?' Alfie was asking. 'Is that nice? Wouldn't that look good in the front room, in the 'allway, in that little alcove 'alfway up the stairs?'

People were nodding, some of their hands already going to their pockets. And Wendy stood there as if she'd been turned into glass herself; big eyes, mouth wide open.

'Perfect in every detail, girl,' he said to a woman in the front. 'And 'ere's 'is sister.' Quickly, he tore the tissue off the twin figure from the box. More clucks, and no one moving. 'Now, young lady, you tell me, are these nice or aren't they?' And before Wendy could do anything about it, even if she'd wanted to, Alfie had given Charlie a figure and he was handing it over for Wendy to hold.

Everyone turned round, the way people do, to see the look on her face.

She took the figure; she held it; she looked at it; she even, very nearly, stroked it; and then she looked back at Alfie Cox.

He'd been right. He definitely knew how to get at her, even against her will. Wendy and her blue glass. I'd seen her face; I was looking at it now; and now I knew all the temptations good-looking Alfie could throw at her – the trouble he could make, here in front of everyone and anywhere we went around Thames Reach.

And he was using an old market trick. Get someone to hold what you're selling till you've finished. No one walks away till they see whether or not the person buys it – and especially not the person herself.

'An' I'll tell you what,' he was going on, 'you can forget twelve pound . . .'

It was a clever, cocky bit of performing: Alfie Cox all full of himself, loving the spotlight, using his soap box to push himself between Wendy and me.

'An' you can forget a tenner . . .'

And suddenly I snapped. God alive, that was enough! I couldn't stand and watch him doing it another second, the flash Handsome Harry! All out to show her what a catch he was, what he could give her if he wanted to. Well, he wasn't going to have it all his own way. He wasn't the only one with decent stuff to sell or give away. For a start, that stuff Max was making didn't come in a thousand identical boxes, like his blue glass. That was unique. And if he could shout the odds about his mass-made stuff, what about me and our really good gear? Too right! What was more, *I'd worked it all out, hadn't I?* I knew the words. There was no way I'd get thrown by drying-up this time. Hell, I might not be big enough to hit Alfie Cox, but now I'd take my chance and stand up to shout the odds against him any day of the week. And especially today.

And I was glad the Big Fellow wasn't around just yet, because that only left me to do it. And I *could* do it. I knew I could. My heart was really thumping with the excitement of it: getting up, taking a chance, putting my head back and trying some new note I'd never reached before.

'Not nine pound, not even eight,' Alfie was going on.

It'd be that midnight-blue handbag Max had finished, that's what I'd use; and I could go on to the matching fashion waistcoats; get to the girls in the crowd. After that, there was a ton of stuff: and the words would come, I knew they would. It'd be like writing a song.

I reached for the handbag, unhooked it. Took two steps up on to the box.

'Kevin! What you doing, Kevin? Kevin, get down for cris-sake!'

Max was pulling at my leg; but I'd got that opening sentence buzzing over in my brain. My inside didn't belong to me, I'd run out of breath without opening my mouth – but I knew it'd be there when I wanted it. I knew I could make it. I knew I *wanted* to make it.

And I knew the answer to what had been bugging me since Tuesday. Yes, I was like the Big Fellow, I wanted to be like him; and I did have the chemistry.

And knowing it suddenly stopped me short – because all of a sudden I could see that knowing it was good enough. I didn't have a thing to prove to anyone now I'd proved it to myself. I'd answered my own question, and I was the only one who needed to know what that answer was.

I jumped down off the stall and pushed my way through the crowd to Wendy. She'd seen me coming. She'd turned away from Alfie and she was smiling at me. The old smile.

I took the figure from her. 'Do these bounce an' all?' I shouted; and I threw the little blue man at Alfie.

He caught it; nearly dropped the others he'd got in his hands to do it, but he caught it. And he swore.

'Come on,' I said to Wendy. '*I'll* stand on your landing for nothing if you like!'

'You're on!' She squeezed me round the waist, and with a nice, polite goodbye smile to Alfie, she edged away with me.

'Thought I saw you getting up just now. For a minute I thought you were going to . . .'

'Slang it out with him? No way. Listen, if you're not coming for a burger for the pleasure of my company, you're not coming for the brilliance of my performance on a soap-box.'

She didn't say a word, couldn't, as we pushed through the crowd.

'Anyway, have you got long?' I asked her.

She laughed. 'Couldn't tell you. That rotten watch of yours – it goes backwards!'

I laughed, too. 'Oh, shame! Tell you what I'll get you another one when I can afford it.' I thought for a second. 'How about something with a blue glass face?'

'Now that *would* be nice.'

We found a bit of space and headed for the Wimpy, holding hands. My feet didn't seem to touch the ground, and it wasn't the rotting cabbage leaves this time. It was Wendy. It was life.

Quietly, so that no one else could hear, I started humming the beginnings of a tune. Faster, more up-tempo than 'High Pavement Blues', something that'd stretch me even more when I got back to playing the Hohner: a tune from way back that seemed just right for now.

'Is that something I ought to know?' Wendy mocked me. 'Has Sinatra done it?'

'I don't reckon,' I said. 'It's the Big Fellow's; just come back to me.'

'What's it called?'

I stopped. 'What's it called? It's called, "You Can Have Your Cake and Eat It If You Try". Just a tune. Up to now. But you never know, I might put some words to it, sometime.' And I gave her a hug and walked us off for a burger.

THE VILLAGE BY THE SEA
Anita Desai

Hari and his sister Lila are the eldest children of an Indian family. Their mother is ill and their father spends most of his time in a drunken stupor. Grimly, Lila and Hari struggle to hold the family together until one day, in a last-ditch attempt to break out of this poverty, Hari leaves his sisters in the silent, shadowy hut and runs off to Bombay. How Hari and Lila cope with the harsh realities of life in city and village is vividly described in this moving and powerful story.

BREAK OF DARK
Robert Westall

A haunted bomber plane, a very odd hitchhiker, an ordinary policeman faced with a series of extraordinary thefts: Robert Westall's chilling stories show just how eerily the supernatural can cross over into the everyday world.

Also in Puffin Plus

A PROPER LITTLE NOORYEFF
Jean Ure

Jamie was a fool. A dolt. A clod. A weak-kneed, lily-livered, yellow-bellied clod. Why couldn't he say no? It was all his little sister's fault – if she hadn't insisted that he meet her after Ballet classes, he'd be playing cricket for his school instead of prancing about in a pair of tights. And what if the mob from Tenterden Road Comprehensive found out?

EASY CONNECTIONS
Liz Berry

Some people say Cathy is a brilliant painter with an exceptional future ahead of her. But from the day when she unwittingly trespasses on the country estate of rock star Paul Devlin, she becomes a changed character. Beautiful, cold and violent, Dev is captivated by Cathy, while she is attracted and repelled in equal measures. However, Dev usually gets what he wants . . .

An unusual love story set in the vivid worlds of rock music and art.

Also in Puffin Plus

LET THE CIRCLE BE UNBROKEN
Mildred D. Taylor

For Cassie Logan, 1935 in the American deep south is a time of bewildering change: the Depression is tightening its grip, rich and poor are in conflict and racial tension is increasing. As she grows away from the security of childhood, Cassie struggles to understand the turmoil around her and the reasons for the deep-rooted fears of her family and friends.

A FOREIGN AFFAIR
John Rowe Townsend

It doesn't seem like a promising party, but when best-looking boy in the room – the Crown Pri Essenheim – seeks her out, Kate is flattered. But it c a blow when he appears equally interested in her political journalist. On hearing rumours of an im revolution in Essenheim, Kate begins to understa dual motive, but little dreams that she too has a v play in the future of that country. A funny and story about affairs of state and affairs of the he

Also in Plus

THE VILLAGE BY THE SEA
Anita Desai

Hari and his sister Lila are the eldest children of an Indian family. Their mother is ill and their father spends most of his time in a drunken stupor. Grimly, Lila and Hari struggle to hold the family together until one day, in a last-ditch attempt to break out of this poverty, Hari leaves his sisters in the silent, shadowy hut and runs off to Bombay. How Hari and Lila cope with the harsh realities of life in city and village is vividly described in this moving and powerful story.

BREAK OF DARK
Robert Westall

A haunted bomber plane, a very odd hitchhiker, an ordinary policeman faced with a series of extraordinary thefts: Robert Westall's chilling stories show just how eerily the supernatural can cross over into the everyday world.

Also in Puffin Plus

A PROPER LITTLE NOORYEFF
Jean Ure

Jamie was a fool. A dolt. A clod. A weak-kneed, lily-livered, yellow-bellied clod. Why couldn't he say no? It was all his little sister's fault – if she hadn't insisted that he meet her after Ballet classes, he'd be playing cricket for his school instead of prancing about in a pair of tights. And what if the mob from Tenterden Road Comprehensive found out?

EASY CONNECTIONS
Liz Berry

Some people say Cathy is a brilliant painter with an exceptional future ahead of her. But from the day when she unwittingly trespasses on the country estate of rock star Paul Devlin, she becomes a changed character. Beautiful, cold and violent, Dev is captivated by Cathy, while she is attracted and repelled in equal measures. However, Dev usually gets what he wants . . .

An unusual love story set in the vivid worlds of rock music and art.

LET THE CIRCLE BE UNBROKEN
Mildred D. Taylor

For Cassie Logan, 1935 in the American deep south is a time of bewildering change: the Depression is tightening its grip, rich and poor are in conflict and racial tension is increasing. As she grows away from the security of childhood, Cassie struggles to understand the turmoil around her and the reasons for the deep-rooted fears of her family and friends.

A FOREIGN AFFAIR
John Rowe Townsend

It doesn't seem like a promising party, but when the best-looking boy in the room – the Crown Prince of Essenheim – seeks her out, Kate is flattered. But it comes as a blow when he appears equally interested in her father, a political journalist. On hearing rumours of an impending revolution in Essenheim, Kate begins to understand Rudi's dual motive, but little dreams that she too has a vital part to play in the future of that country. A funny and fast paced story about affairs of state and affairs of the heart.